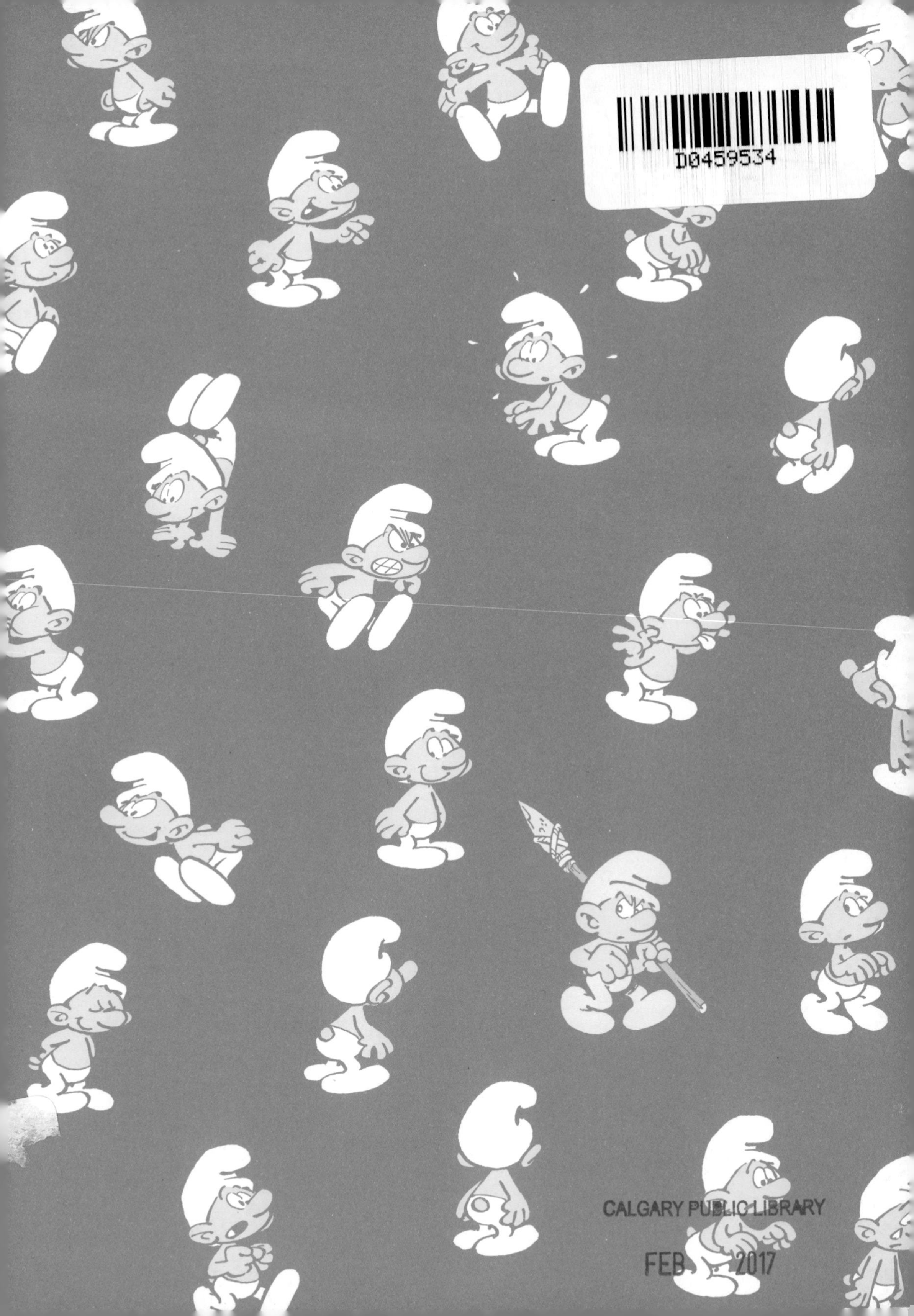

THE SMURF MENACE

Peyo

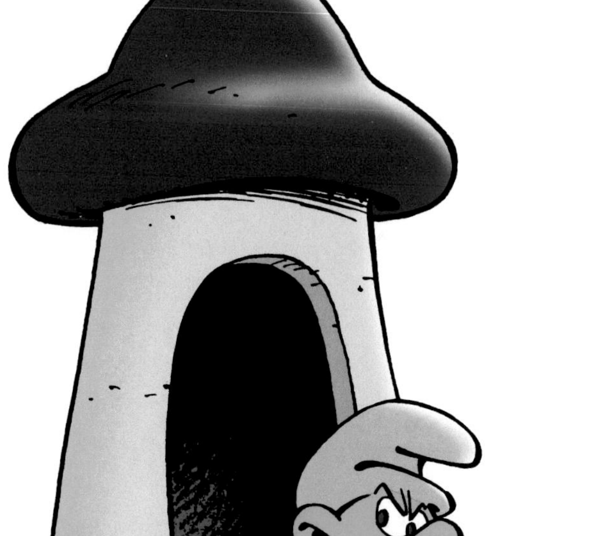

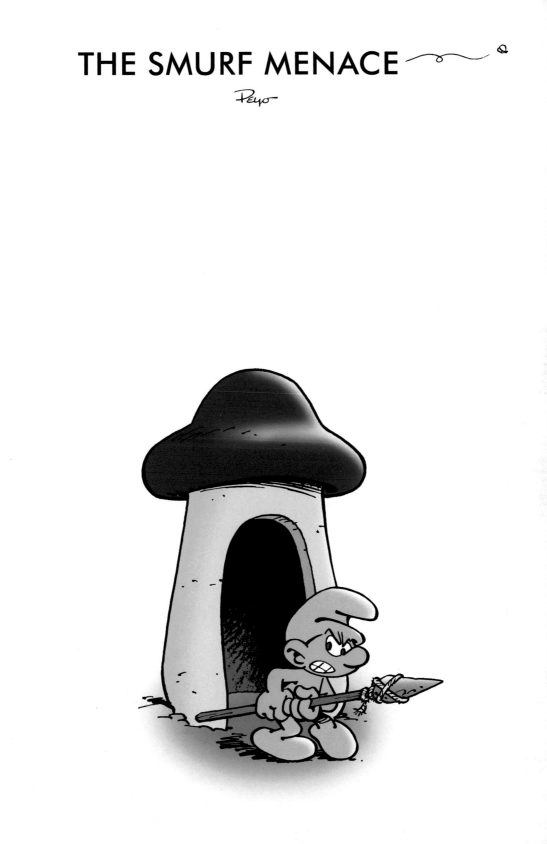

THE SMURF MENACE

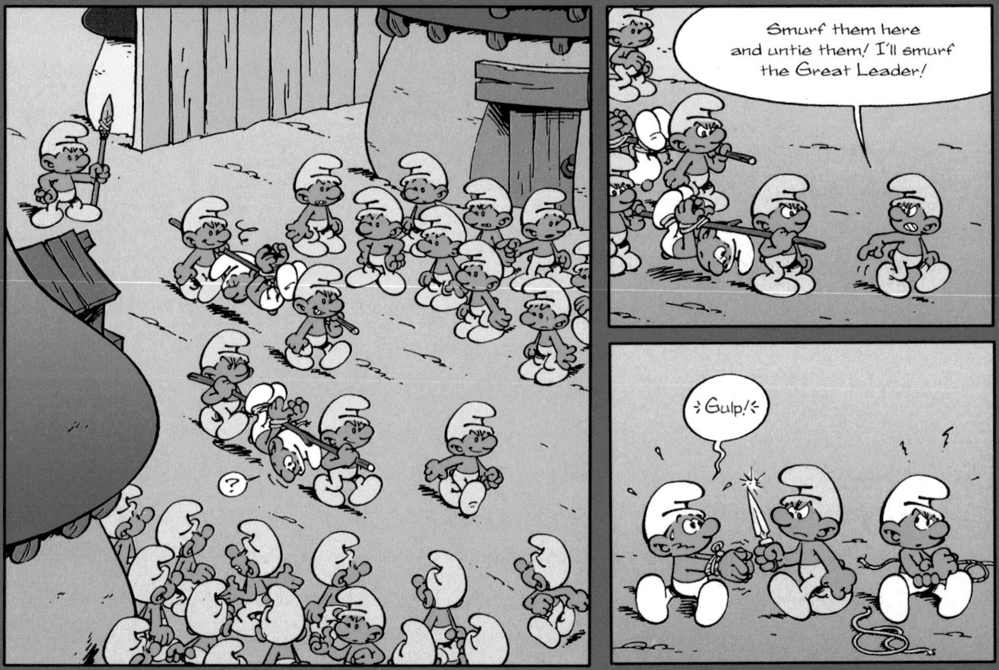

?
Smurf them here and untie them! I'll smurf the Great Leader!
Gulp!

A SMURFS GRAPHIC NOVEL BY PEYO

WITH THE COLLABORATION OF
LUC PARTHOENS AND THIERRY CULLIFORD – SCRIPT
ALAIN MAURY AND LUC PARTHOENS – ARTWORK
NINE – COLOR

PAPERCUTZ™
NEW YORK

SMURFS GRAPHIC NOVELS AVAILABLE FROM PAPERCUTZ™

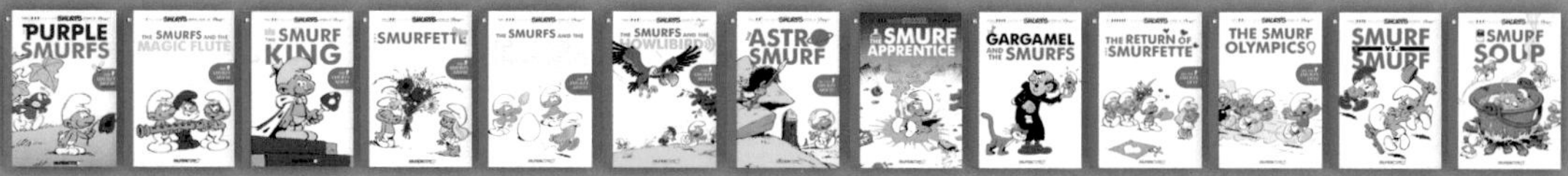

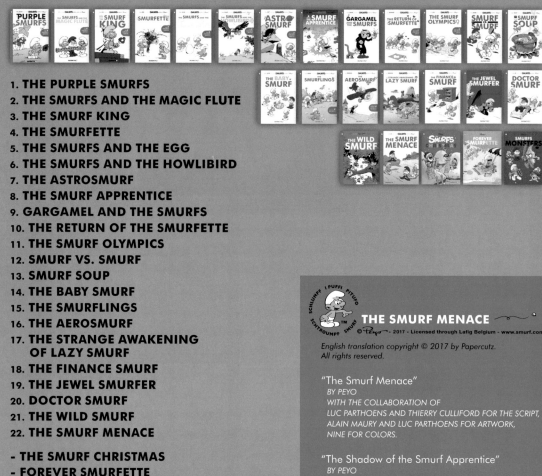

PURPLE SMURFS
THE SMURFS AND THE MAGIC FLUTE
THE SMURF KING
SMURFETTE
ASTRO SMURF
SMURF APPRENTICE
GARGAMEL AND THE SMURFS
THE RETURN OF THE SMURFETTE
THE SMURF OLYMPICS
SMURF SOUP

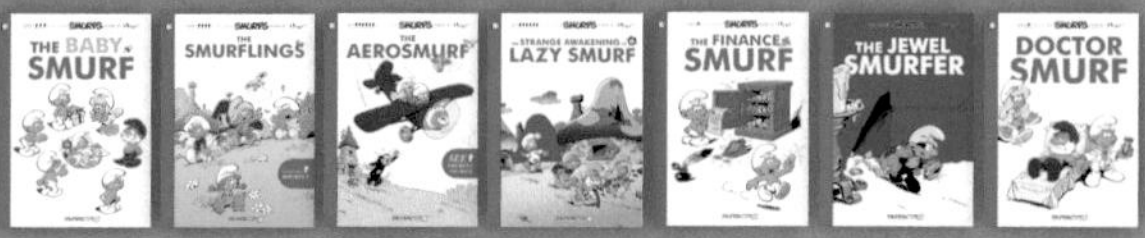

THE BABY SMURF
SMURFLINGS
AEROSMURF
LAZY SMURF
THE FINANCE SMURF
THE JEWEL SMURFER
DOCTOR SMURF

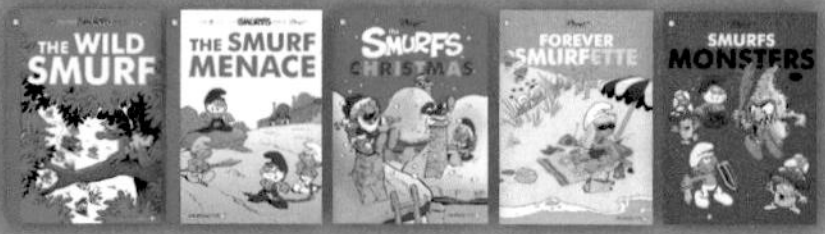

THE WILD SMURF
THE SMURF MENACE
SMURFS
FOREVER SMURFETTE
SMURFS MONSTERS

1. THE PURPLE SMURFS
2. THE SMURFS AND THE MAGIC FLUTE
3. THE SMURF KING
4. THE SMURFETTE
5. THE SMURFS AND THE EGG
6. THE SMURFS AND THE HOWLIBIRD
7. THE ASTROSMURF
8. THE SMURF APPRENTICE
9. GARGAMEL AND THE SMURFS
10. THE RETURN OF THE SMURFETTE
11. THE SMURF OLYMPICS
12. SMURF VS. SMURF
13. SMURF SOUP
14. THE BABY SMURF
15. THE SMURFLINGS
16. THE AEROSMURF
17. THE STRANGE AWAKENING OF LAZY SMURF
18. THE FINANCE SMURF
19. THE JEWEL SMURFER
20. DOCTOR SMURF
21. THE WILD SMURF
22. THE SMURF MENACE

- THE SMURF CHRISTMAS
- FOREVER SMURFETTE
- SMURFS MONSTERS

THE SMURFS graphic novels are available in paperback for $5.99 each and in hardcover for $10.99 each, except for THE SMURFS #21 and #22, which are $7.99 in paperback and $12.99 in hardcover, at booksellers everywhere. You can also order online at papercutz.com. Or call 1-800-886-1223, Monday through Friday, 9 – 5 EST. MC, Visa, and AmEx accepted. To order by mail, please add $4.00 for postage and handling for first book ordered, $1.00 for each additional book and make check payable to NBM Publishing. Send to: Papercutz, 160 Broadway, Suite 700, East Wing, New York, NY 10038.

THE SMURFS graphic novels are also available digitally wherever e-books are sold.

PAPERCUTZ.COM

THE SMURF MENACE

"The Smurf Menace"
BY PEYO
WITH THE COLLABORATION OF
LUC PARTHOENS AND THIERRY CULLIFORD FOR THE SCRIPT,
ALAIN MAURY AND LUC PARTHOENS FOR ARTWORK,
NINE FOR COLORS.

"The Shadow of the Smurf Apprentice"
BY PEYO

"The Mansion of a Thousand Mirrors"
BY PEYO

Joe Johnson, *SMURFLATIONS*
Adam Grano, *SMURFIC DESIGN*
Janice Chiang, *LETTERING SMURFETTE*
Matt. Murray, *SMURF CONSULTANT*
Rachel Pinnelas, *SMURF COORDINATOR*
Jeff Whitman, *ASSISTANT MANAGING SMURF*
Jim Salicrup, *SMURF-IN-CHIEF*

PAPERBACK EDITION ISBN: 978-1-62991-622-4
HARDCOVER EDITION ISBN: 978-1-62991-623-1

PRINTED IN CHINA JANUARY 2017 BY WKT CO. LTD.

Papercutz books may be purchased for business or promotional use. For information on bulk purchases please contact Macmillan Corporate and Premium Sales Department at (800) 221-7945 x5442.

DISTRIBUTED BY MACMILLAN
FIRST PAPERCUTZ PRINTING

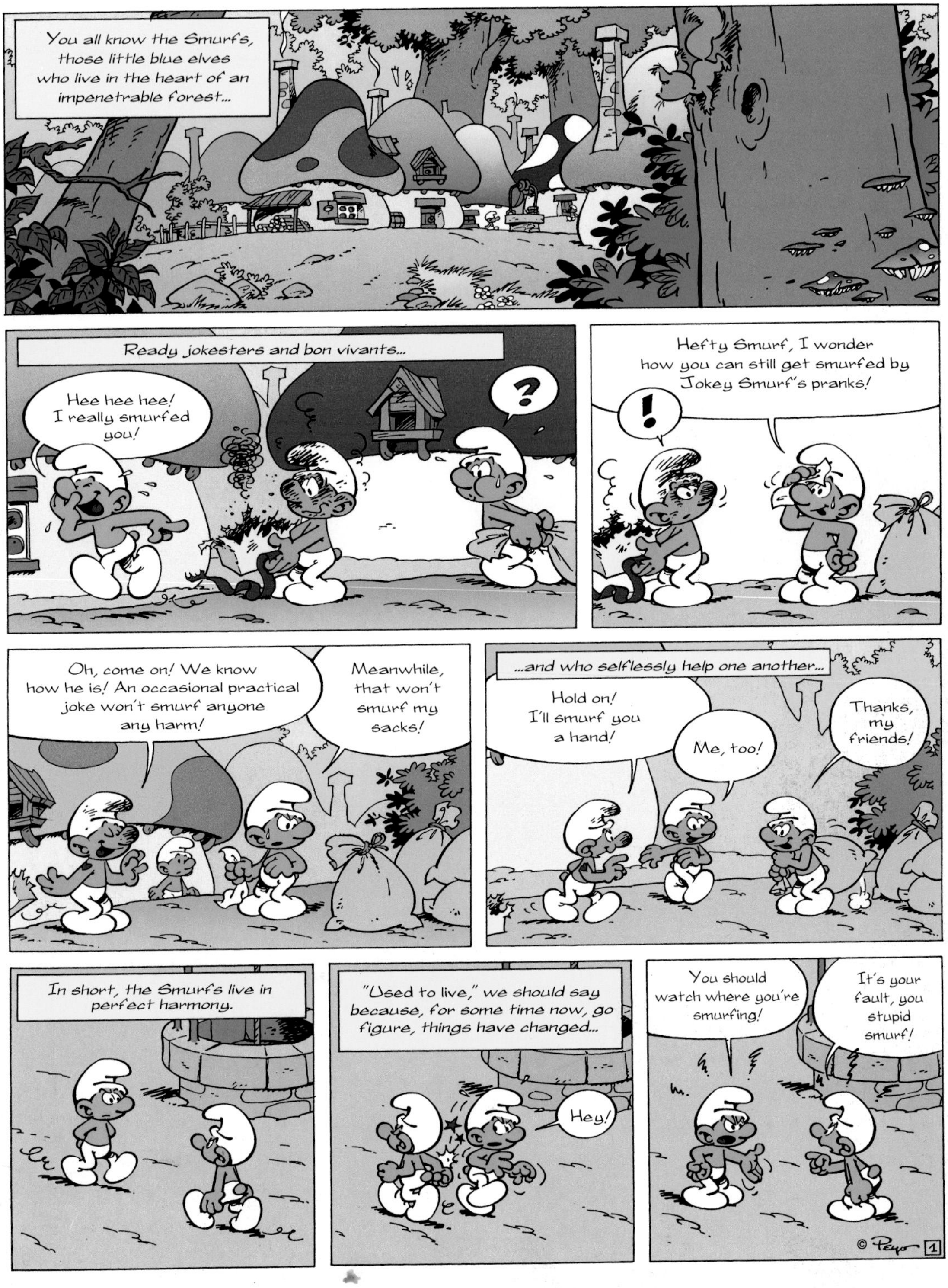
You all know the Smurfs, those little blue elves who live in the heart of an impenetrable forest...
Ready jokesters and bon vivants...
Hee hee hee! I really smurfed you!
?
Hefty Smurf, I wonder how you can still get smurfed by Jokey Smurf's pranks!
!
Oh, come on! We know how he is! An occasional practical joke won't smurf anyone any harm!
Meanwhile, that won't smurf my sacks!
...and who selflessly help one another...
Hold on! I'll smurf you a hand!
Me, too!
Thanks, my friends!
In short, the Smurfs live in perfect harmony.
"Used to live," we should say because, for some time now, go figure, things have changed...
Hey!
You should watch where you're smurfing!
It's your fault, you stupid smurf!
© Peyo 1

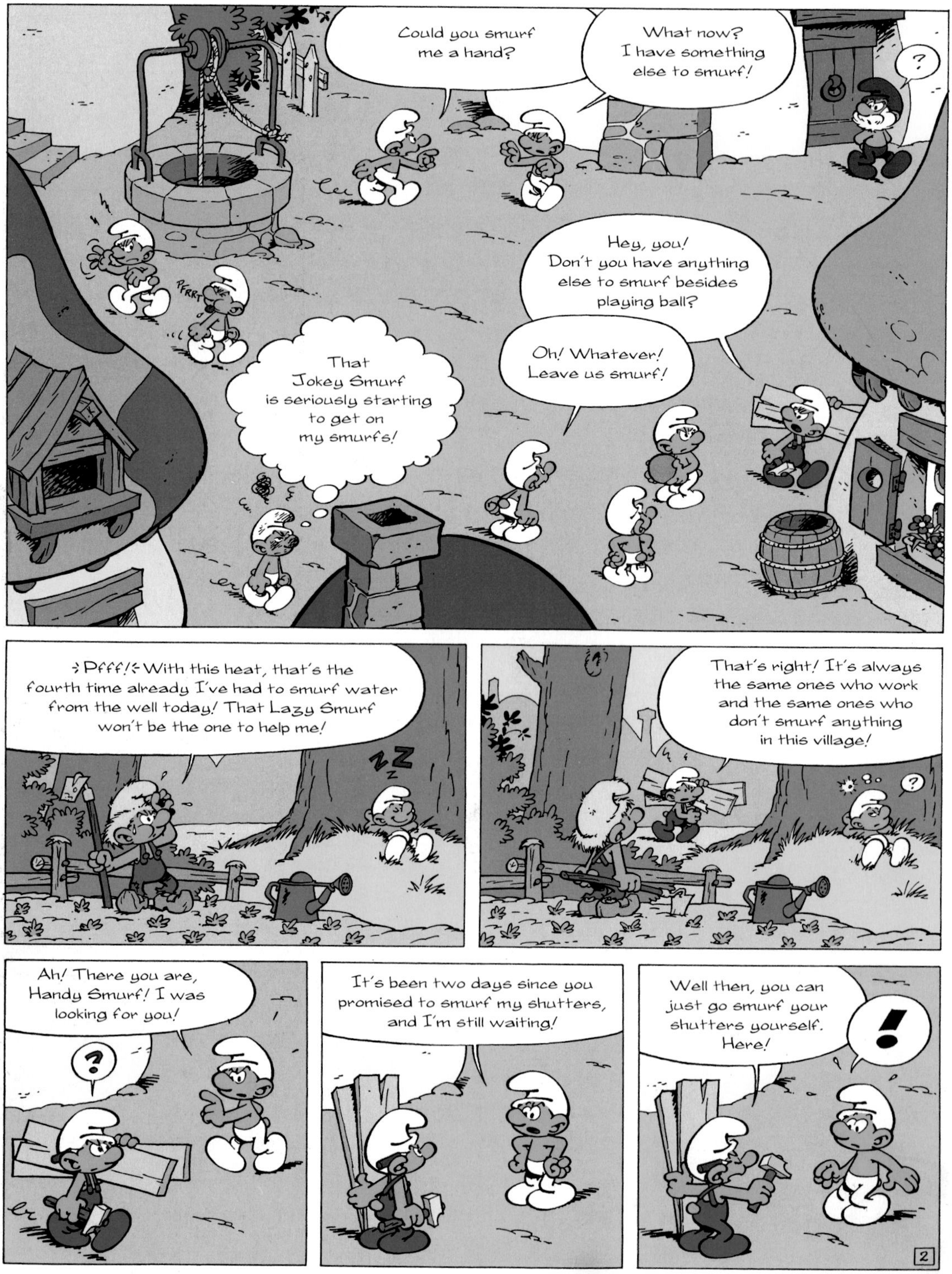
Could you smurf me a hand?
What now? I have something else to smurf!
?
PFFRRT
That Jokey Smurf is seriously starting to get on my smurfs!
Hey, you! Don't you have anything else to smurf besides playing ball?
Oh! Whatever! Leave us smurf!
Pfff! With this heat, that's the fourth time already I've had to smurf water from the well today! That Lazy Smurf won't be the one to help me!
ZZZ
That's right! It's always the same ones who work and the same ones who don't smurf anything in this village!
?
Ah! There you are, Handy Smurf! I was looking for you!
?
It's been two days since you promised to smurf my shutters, and I'm still waiting!
Well then, you can just go smurf your shutters yourself. Here!
!

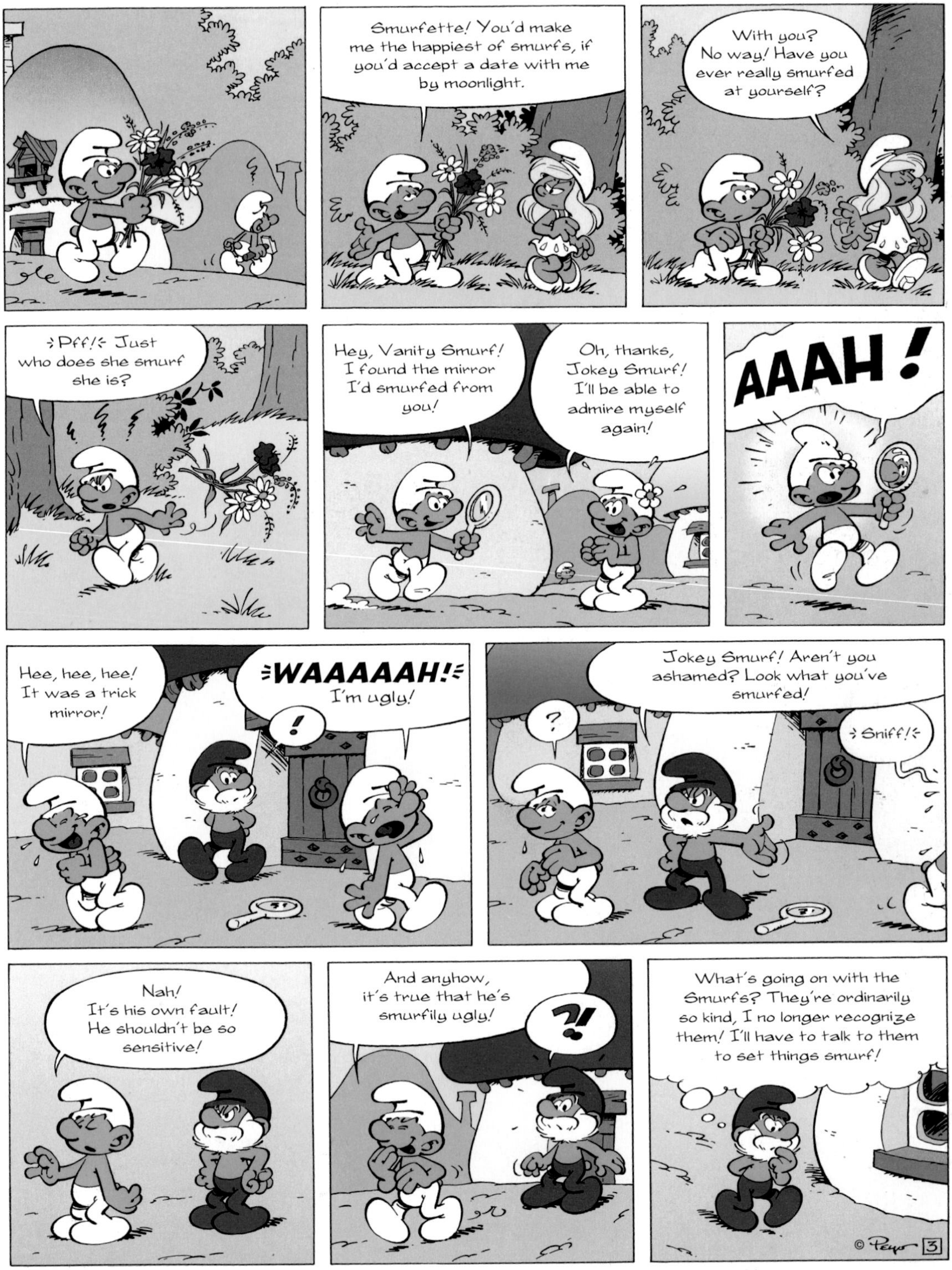
Smurfette! You'd make me the happiest of smurfs, if you'd accept a date with me by moonlight.
With you? No way! Have you ever really smurfed at yourself?
Pff! Just who does she smurf she is?
Hey, Vanity Smurf! I found the mirror I'd smurfed from you!
Oh, thanks, Jokey Smurf! I'll be able to admire myself again!
AAAH!
Hee, hee, hee! It was a trick mirror!
WAAAAAH! I'm ugly!
!
?
Jokey Smurf! Aren't you ashamed? Look what you've smurfed!
Sniff!
Nah! It's his own fault! He shouldn't be so sensitive!
And anyhow, it's true that he's smurfily ugly!
?!
What's going on with the Smurfs? They're ordinarily so kind, I no longer recognize them! I'll have to talk to them to set things smurf!
© Peyo 3

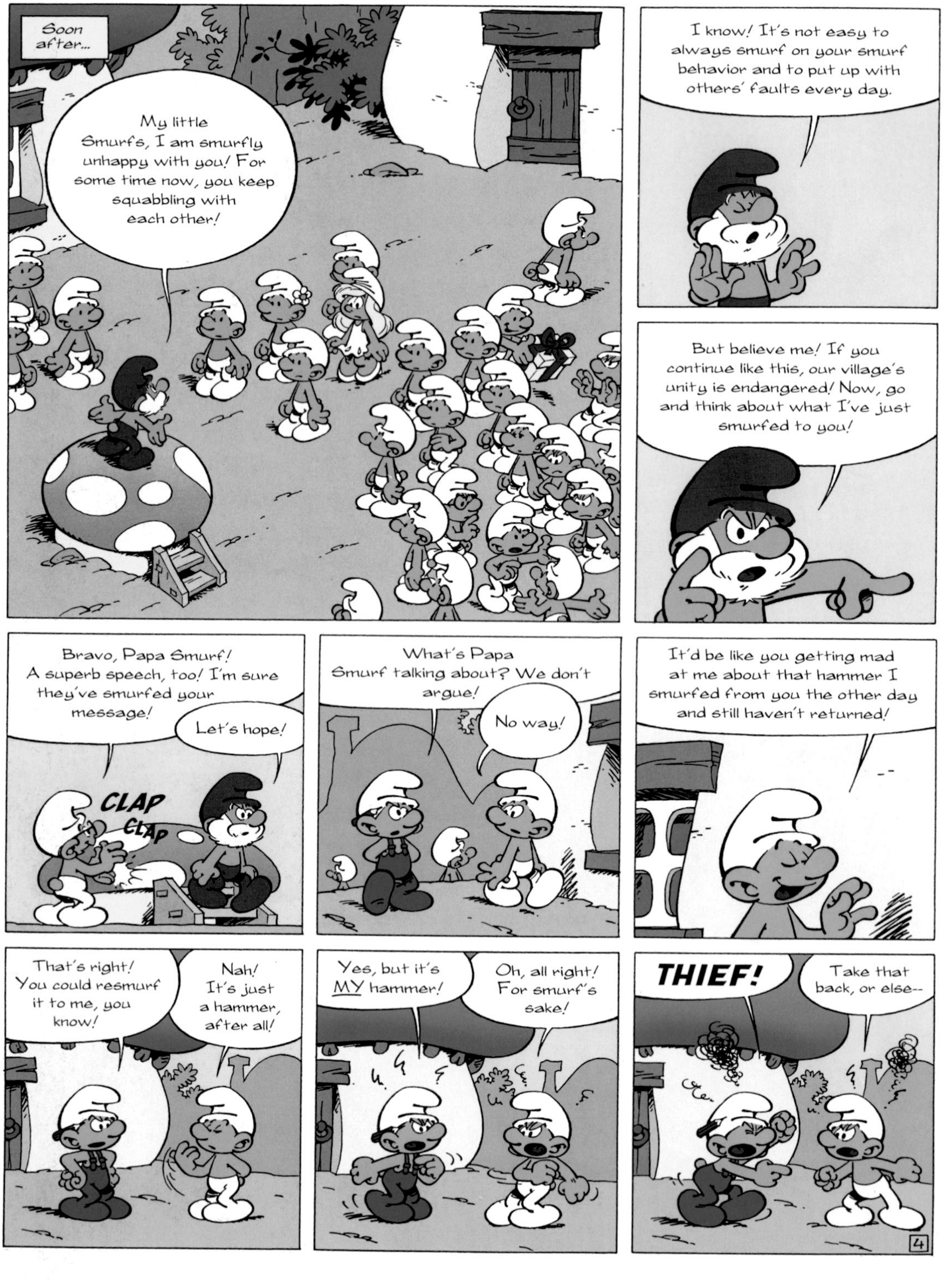

Soon after...
My little Smurfs, I am smurfly unhappy with you! For some time now, you keep squabbling with each other!
I know! It's not easy to always smurf on your smurf behavior and to put up with others' faults every day.
But believe me! If you continue like this, our village's unity is endangered! Now, go and think about what I've just smurfed to you!
Bravo, Papa Smurf! A superb speech, too! I'm sure they've smurfed your message!
Let's hope!
CLAP
CLAP
What's Papa Smurf talking about? We don't argue!
No way!
It'd be like you getting mad at me about that hammer I smurfed from you the other day and still haven't returned!
That's right! You could resmurf it to me, you know!
Nah! It's just a hammer, after all!
Yes, but it's MY hammer!
Oh, all right! For smurf's sake!
THIEF!
Take that back, or else--
4

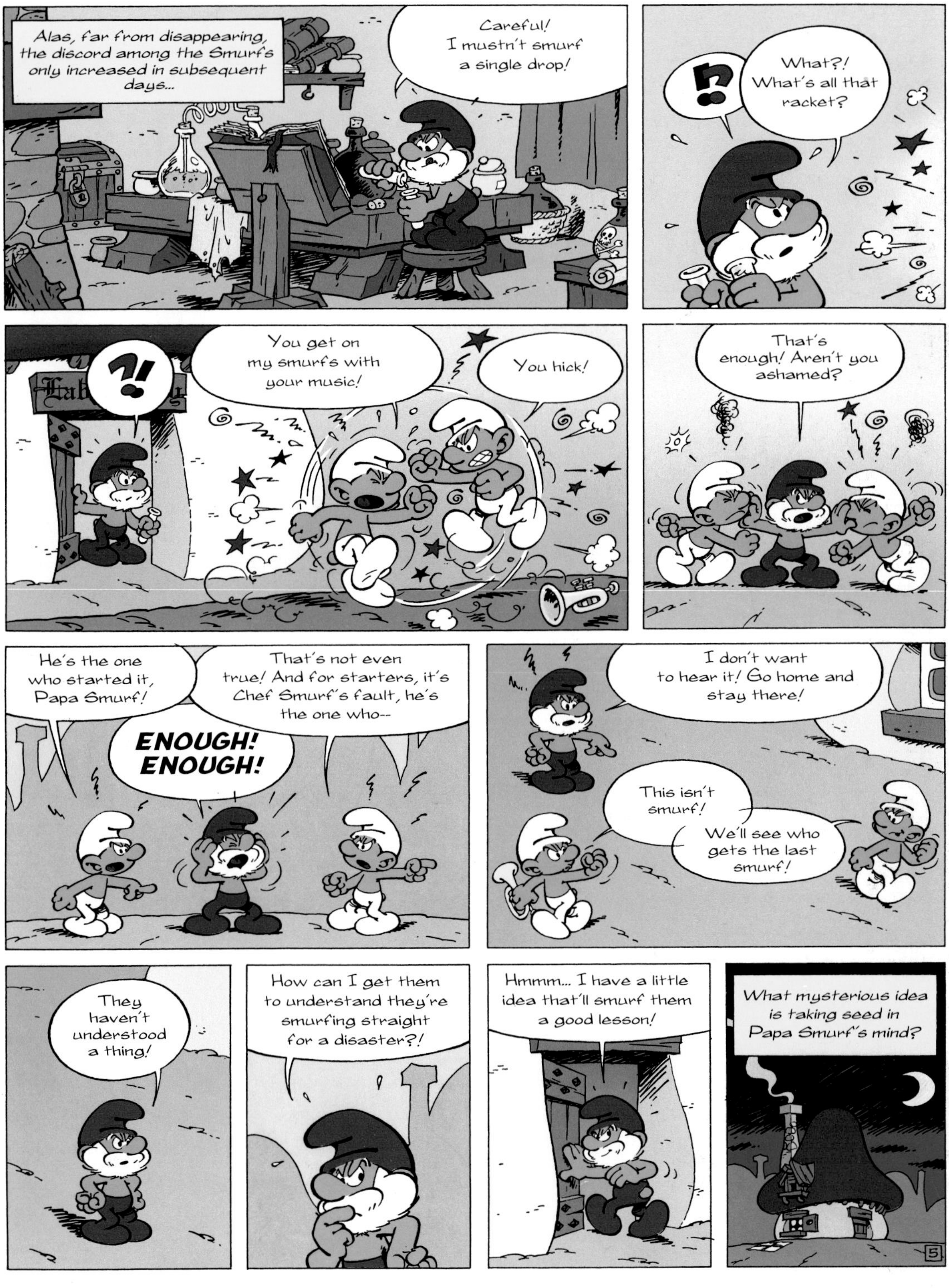

Alas, far from disappearing, the discord among the Smurfs only increased in subsequent days...
Careful! I mustn't smurf a single drop!
?!
What?! What's all that racket?
?!
You get on my smurfs with your music!
You hick!
That's enough! Aren't you ashamed?
He's the one who started it, Papa Smurf!
That's not even true! And for starters, it's Chef Smurf's fault, he's the one who--
ENOUGH! ENOUGH!
I don't want to hear it! Go home and stay there!
This isn't smurf!
We'll see who gets the last smurf!
They haven't understood a thing!
How can I get them to understand they're smurfing straight for a disaster?!
Hmmm... I have a little idea that'll smurf them a good lesson!
What mysterious idea is taking seed in Papa Smurf's mind?
5

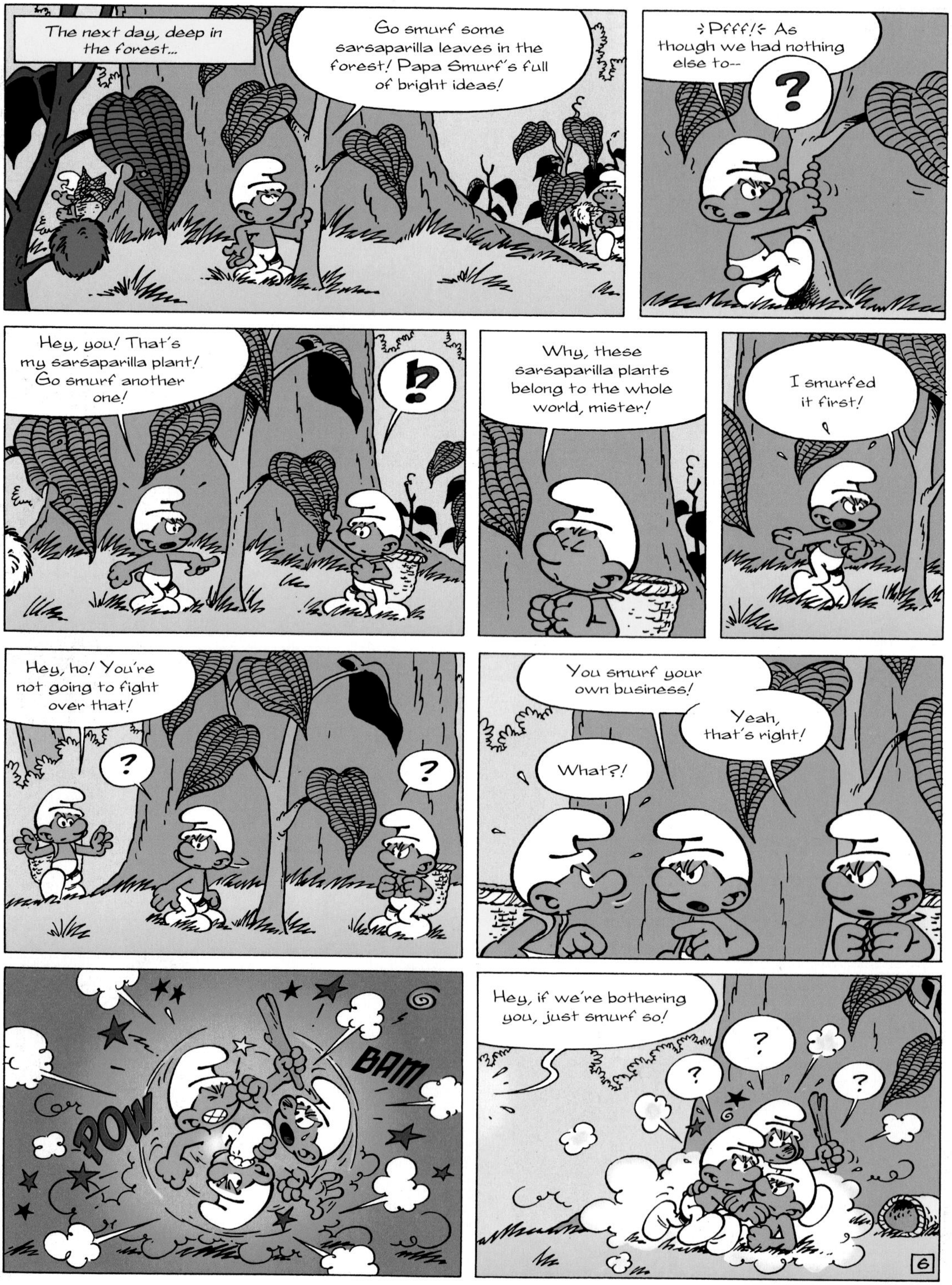

The next day, deep in the forest...
Go smurf some sarsaparilla leaves in the forest! Papa Smurf's full of bright ideas!
Pfff! As though we had nothing else to--
?
Hey, you! That's my sarsaparilla plant! Go smurf another one!
Why, these sarsaparilla plants belong to the whole world, mister!
I smurfed it first!
Hey, ho! You're not going to fight over that!
?
?
You smurf your own business!
Yeah, that's right!
What?!
POW
BAM
Hey, if we're bothering you, just smurf so!
?
?
?
6

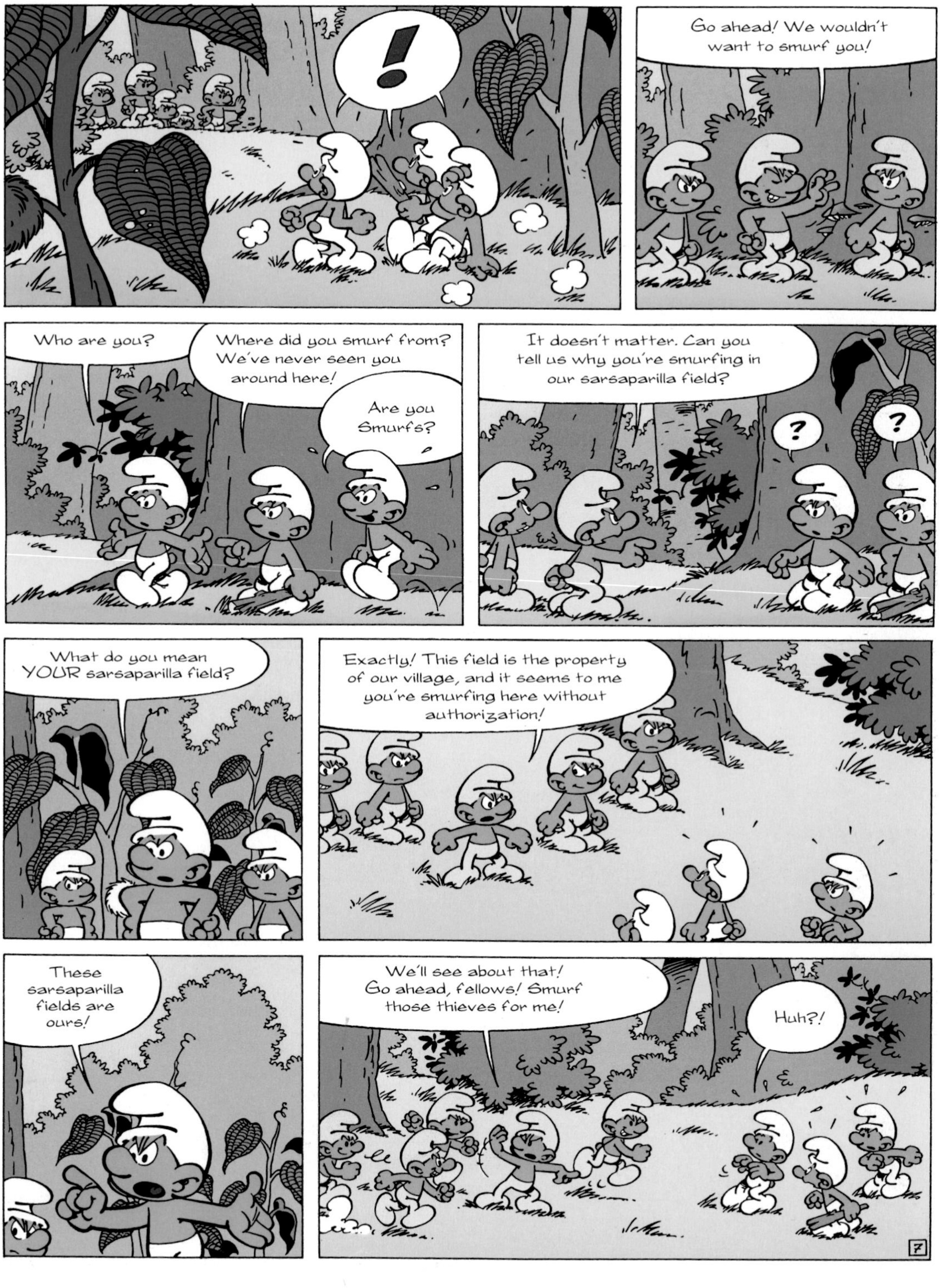
!
Go ahead! We wouldn't want to smurf you!
Who are you?
Where did you smurf from? We've never seen you around here!
Are you Smurfs?
It doesn't matter. Can you tell us why you're smurfing in our sarsaparilla field?
?
?
What do you mean YOUR sarsaparilla field?
Exactly! This field is the property of our village, and it seems to me you're smurfing here without authorization!
These sarsaparilla fields are ours!
We'll see about that! Go ahead, fellows! Smurf those thieves for me!
Huh?!
7

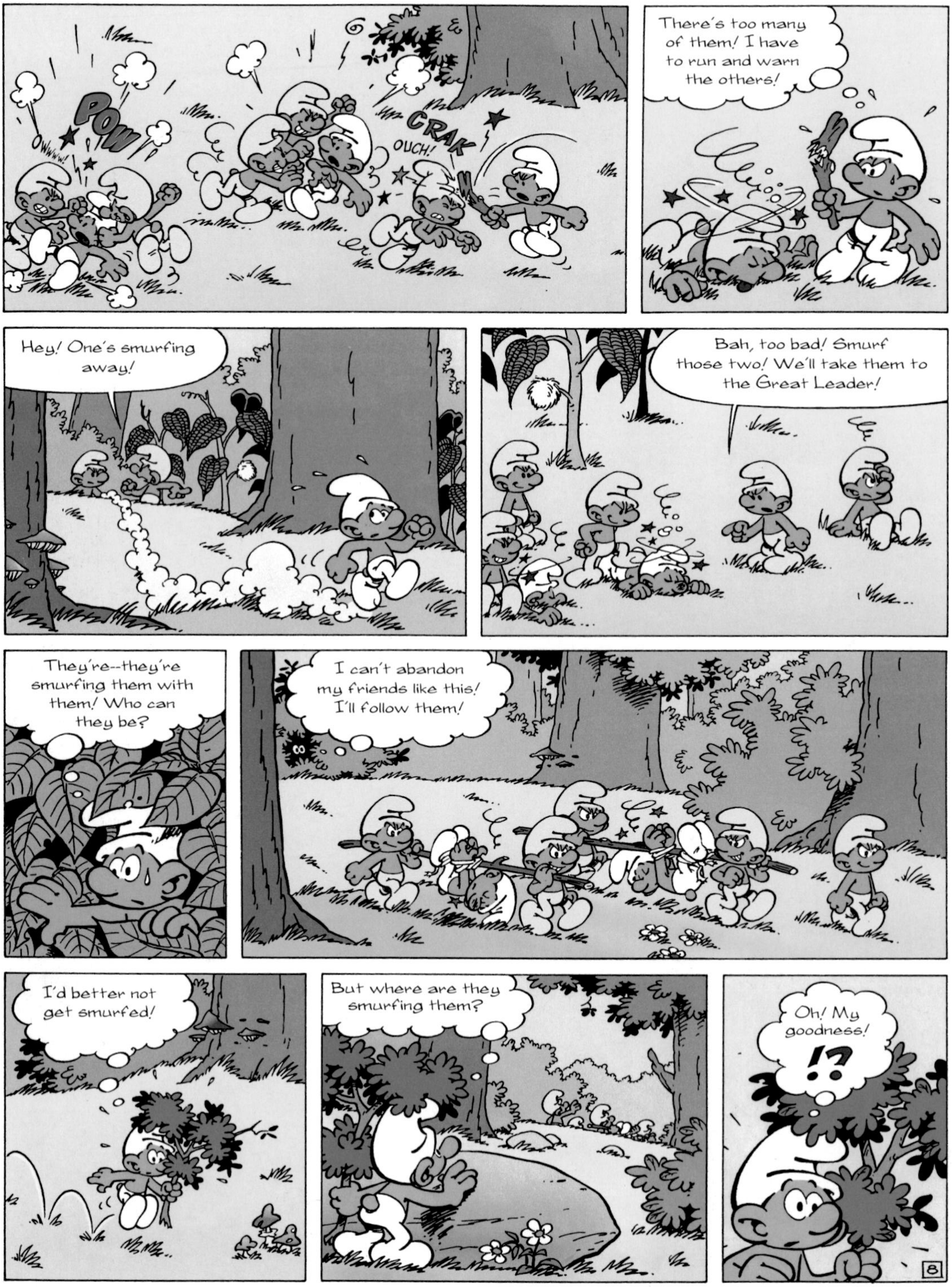

POW
OWWWW!
OUCH!
CRAK
There's too many of them! I have to run and warn the others!
Hey! One's smurfing away!
Bah, too bad! Smurf those two! We'll take them to the Great Leader!
They're--they're smurfing them with them! Who can they be?
I can't abandon my friends like this! I'll follow them!
I'd better not get smurfed!
But where are they smurfing them?
Oh! My goodness!
!?
8

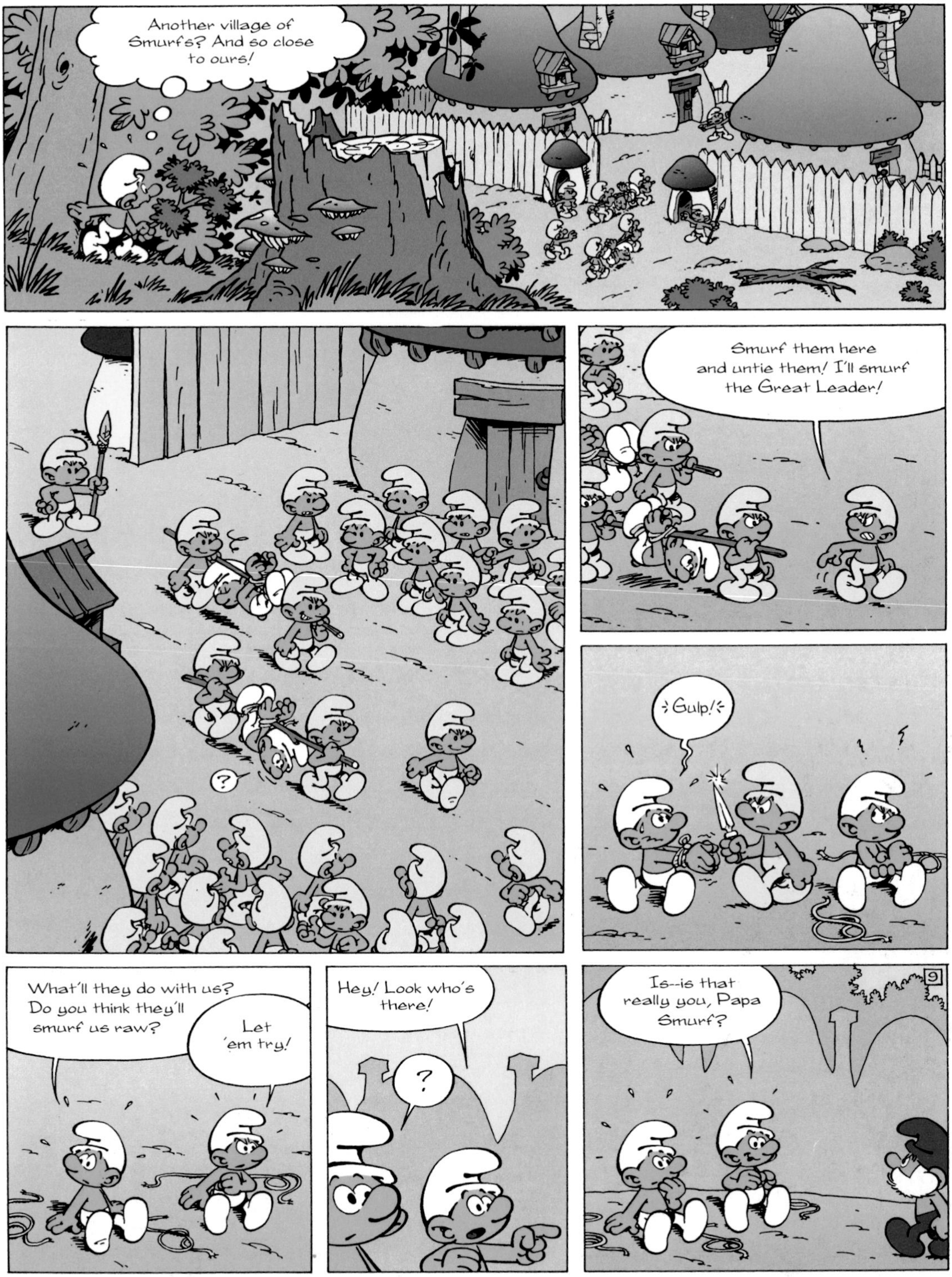

Another village of Smurfs? And so close to ours!
Smurf them here and untie them! I'll smurf the Great Leader!
?
Gulp!
What'll they do with us? Do you think they'll smurf us raw?
Let 'em try!
Hey! Look who's there!
?
Is--is that really you, Papa Smurf?

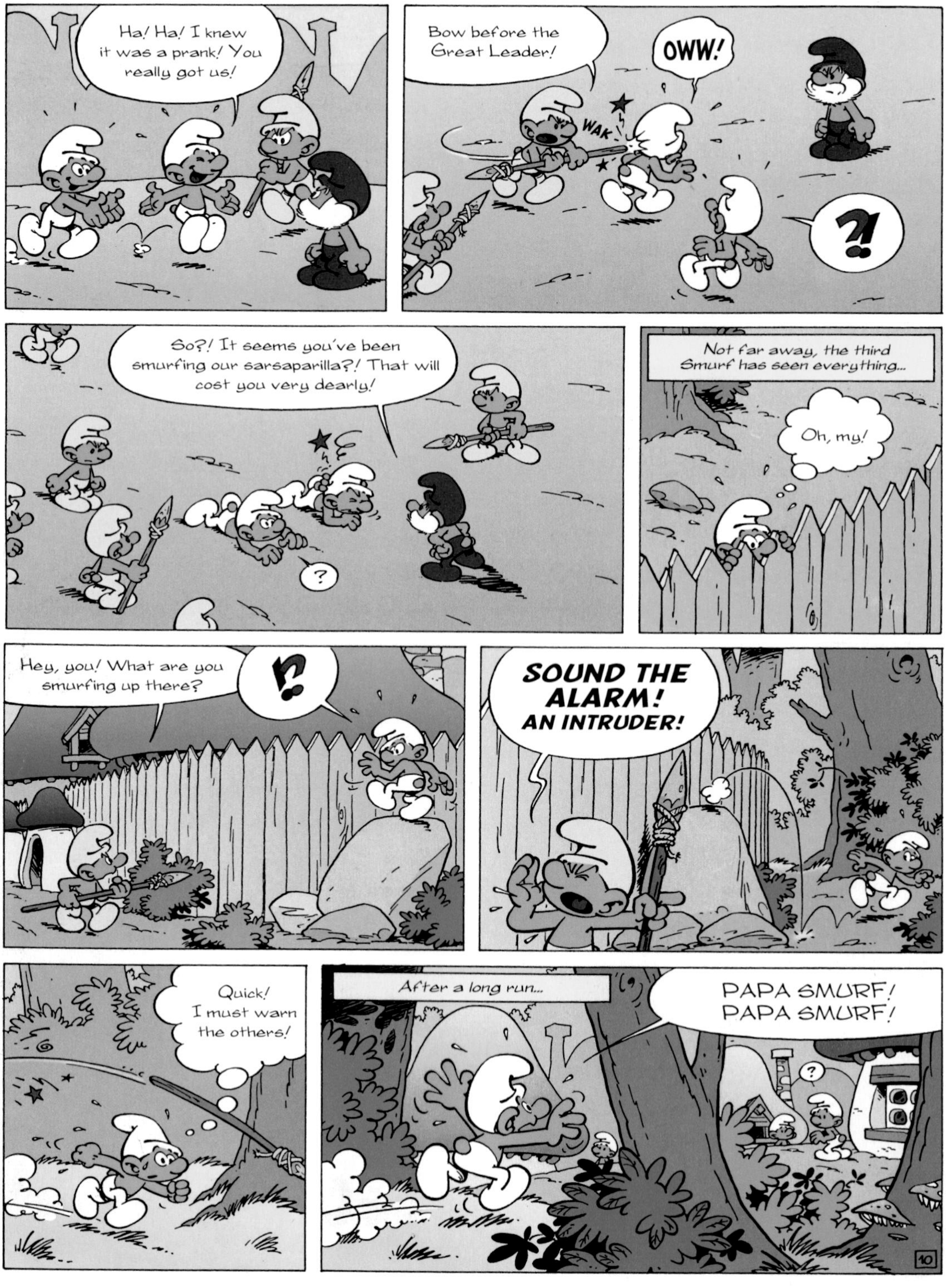

Ha! Ha! I knew it was a prank! You really got us!
Bow before the Great Leader!
OWW!
WAK
?!
So?! It seems you've been smurfing our sarsaparilla?! That will cost you very dearly!
?
Not far away, the third Smurf has seen everything...
Oh, my!
Hey, you! What are you smurfing up there?
!?
SOUND THE ALARM! AN INTRUDER!
Quick! I must warn the others!
After a long run...
PAPA SMURF! PAPA SMURF!
?
10

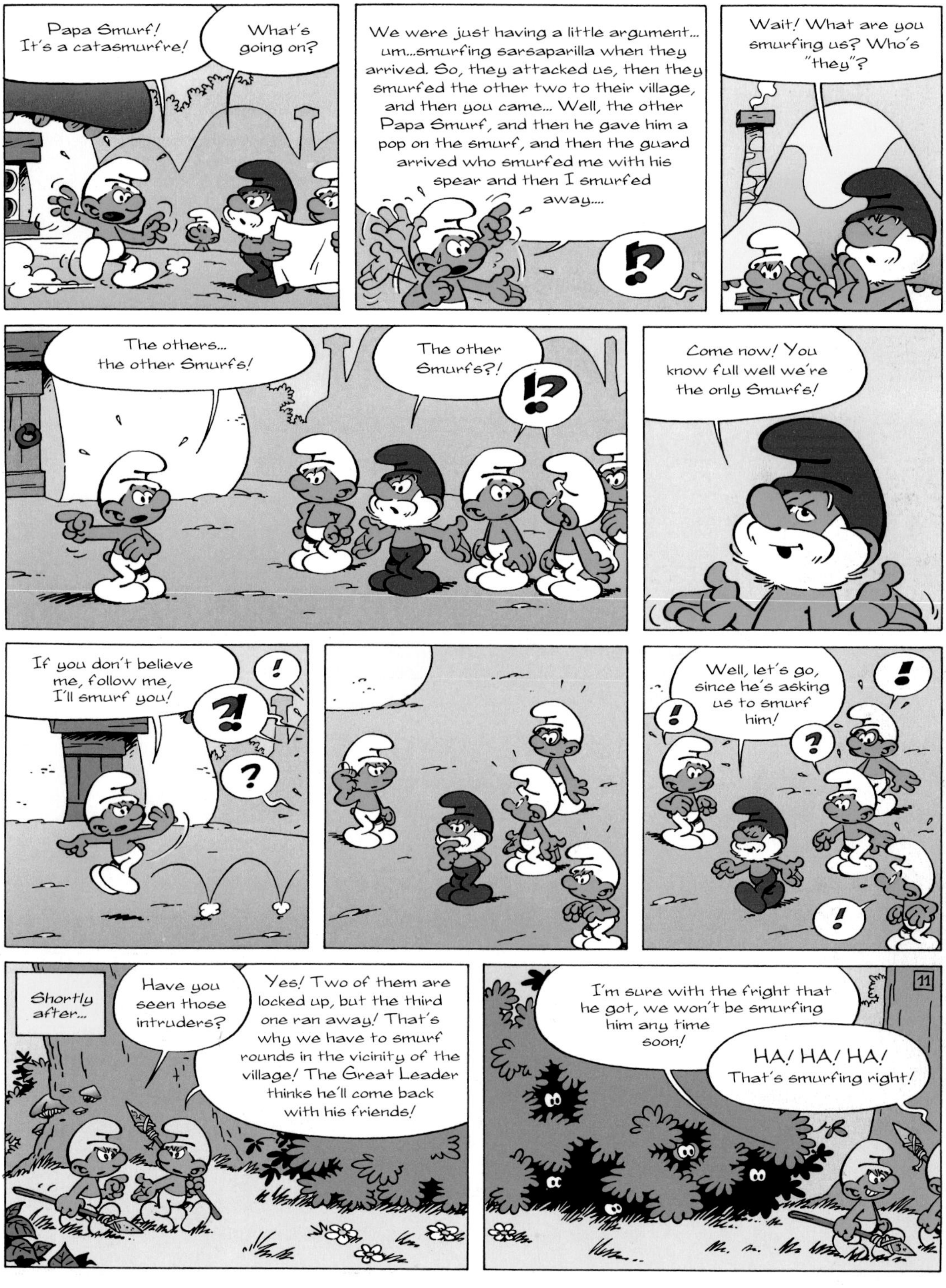
Papa Smurf! It's a catasmurfre!
What's going on?
We were just having a little argument... um...smurfing sarsaparilla when they arrived. So, they attacked us, then they smurfed the other two to their village, and then you came... Well, the other Papa Smurf, and then he gave him a pop on the smurf, and then the guard arrived who smurfed me with his spear and then I smurfed away....
!?
Wait! What are you smurfing us? Who's "they"?
The others... the other Smurfs!
The other Smurfs?!
!?
Come now! You know full well we're the only Smurfs!
If you don't believe me, follow me, I'll smurf you!
!
?!
?
Well, let's go, since he's asking us to smurf him!
!
!
?
!
Shortly after...
Have you seen those intruders?
Yes! Two of them are locked up, but the third one ran away! That's why we have to smurf rounds in the vicinity of the village! The Great Leader thinks he'll come back with his friends!
11
I'm sure with the fright that he got, we won't be smurfing him any time soon!
HA! HA! HA! That's smurfing right!

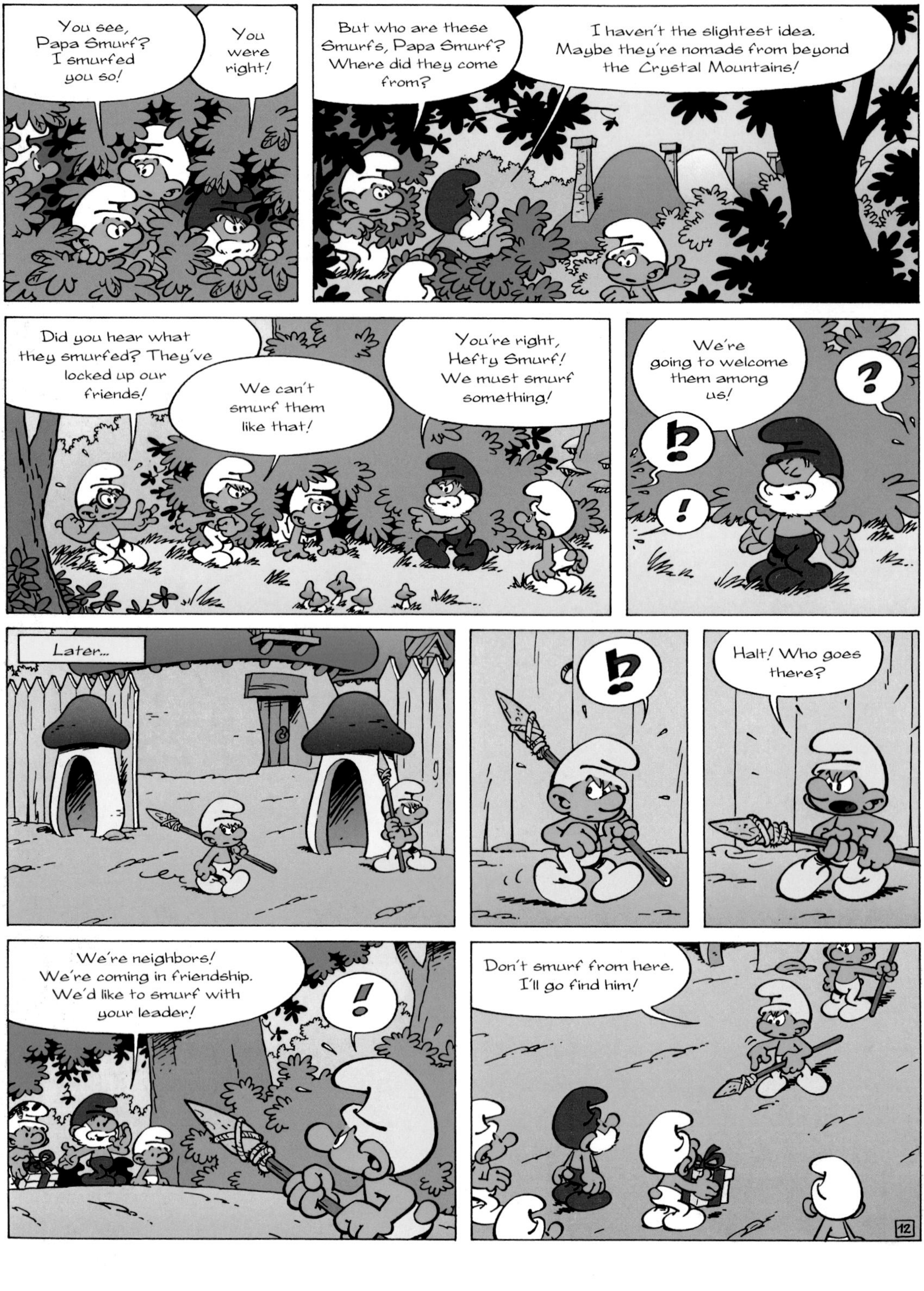
You see, Papa Smurf? I smurfed you so!
You were right!
But who are these Smurfs, Papa Smurf? Where did they come from?
I haven't the slightest idea. Maybe they're nomads from beyond the Crystal Mountains!
Did you hear what they smurfed? They've locked up our friends!
We can't smurf them like that!
You're right, Hefty Smurf! We must smurf something!
We're going to welcome them among us!
?
!?
!
Later...
!?
Halt! Who goes there?
We're neighbors! We're coming in friendship. We'd like to smurf with your leader!
!
Don't smurf from here. I'll go find him!
12

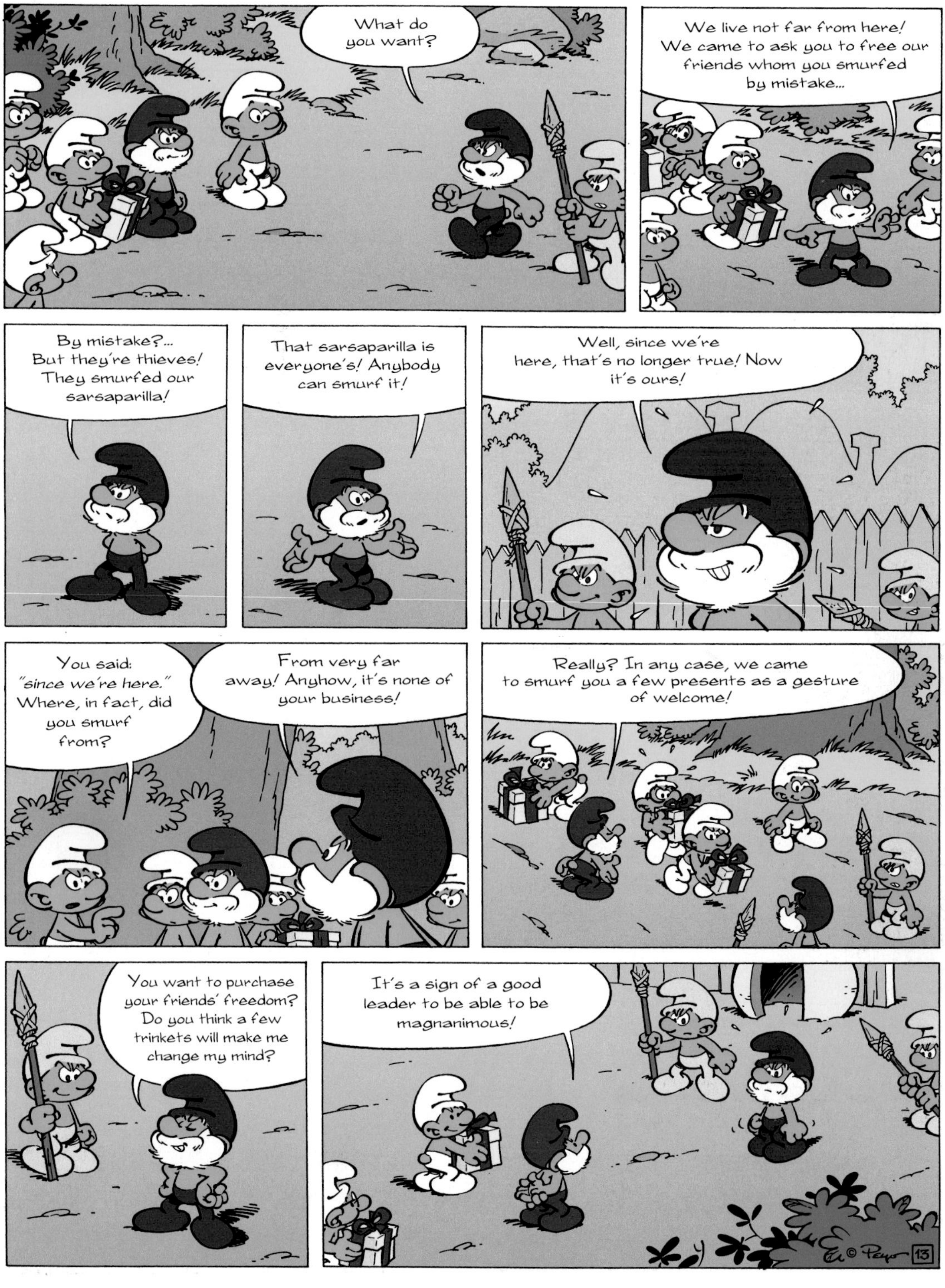
What do you want?
We live not far from here! We came to ask you to free our friends whom you smurfed by mistake...
By mistake?... But they're thieves! They smurfed our sarsaparilla!
That sarsaparilla is everyone's! Anybody can smurf it!
Well, since we're here, that's no longer true! Now it's ours!
You said: "since we're here." Where, in fact, did you smurf from?
From very far away! Anyhow, it's none of your business!
Really? In any case, we came to smurf you a few presents as a gesture of welcome!
You want to purchase your friends' freedom? Do you think a few trinkets will make me change my mind?
It's a sign of a good leader to be able to be magnanimous!
© Peyo
13

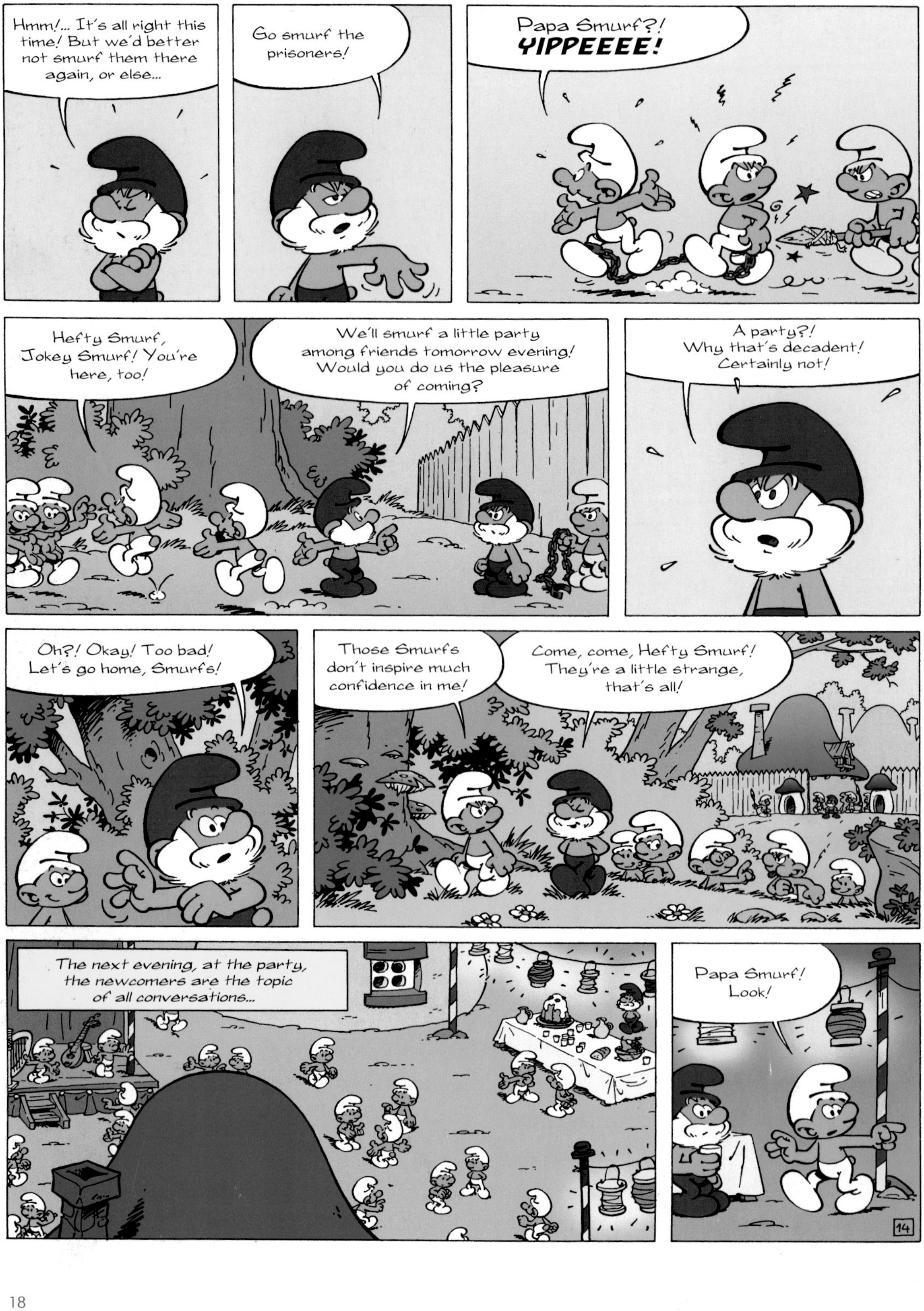
Hmm!... It's all right this time! But we'd better not smurf them there again, or else...
Go smurf the prisoners!
Papa Smurf?! YIPPEEEE!
Hefty Smurf, Jokey Smurf! You're here, too!
We'll smurf a little party among friends tomorrow evening! Would you do us the pleasure of coming?
A party?! Why that's decadent! Certainly not!
Oh?! Okay! Too bad! Let's go home, Smurfs!
Those Smurfs don't inspire much confidence in me!
Come, come, Hefty Smurf! They're a little strange, that's all!
The next evening, at the party, the newcomers are the topic of all conversations...
Papa Smurf! Look!
14

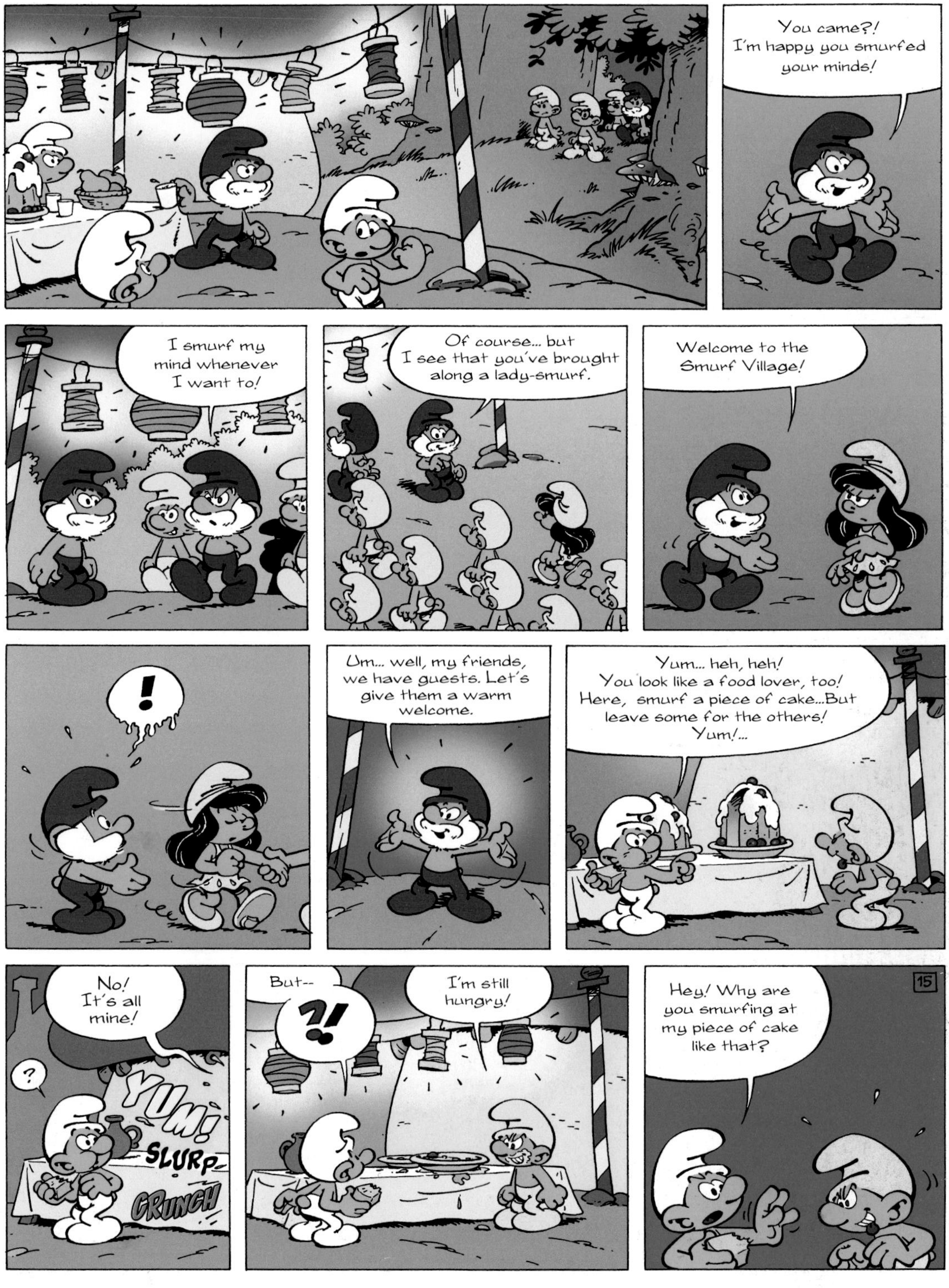
You came?! I'm happy you smurfed your minds!
I smurf my mind whenever I want to!
Of course... but I see that you've brought along a lady-smurf.
Welcome to the Smurf Village!
!
Um... well, my friends, we have guests. Let's give them a warm welcome.
Yum... heh, heh! You look like a food lover, too! Here, smurf a piece of cake...But leave some for the others! Yum!...
No! It's all mine!
?
YUM!
SLURP
CRUNCH
But--
?!
I'm still hungry!
15
Hey! Why are you smurfing at my piece of cake like that?

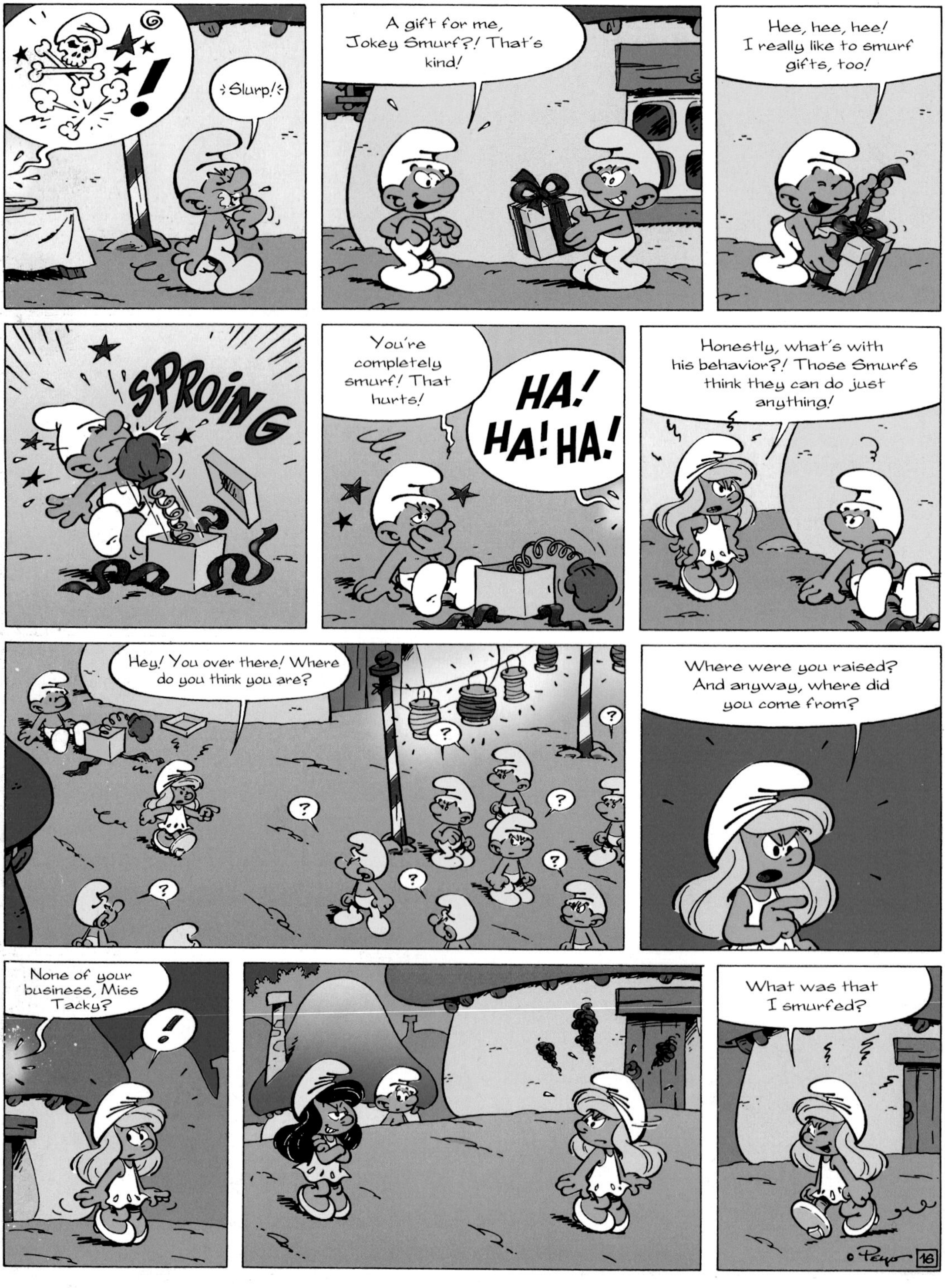

Slurp!
A gift for me, Jokey Smurf?! That's kind!
Hee, hee, hee! I really like to smurf gifts, too!
SPROING
You're completely smurf! That hurts!
HA! HA! HA!
Honestly, what's with his behavior?! Those Smurfs think they can do just anything!
Hey! You over there! Where do you think you are?
Where were you raised? And anyway, where did you come from?
None of your business, Miss Tacky?
What was that I smurfed?
© Peyo
16

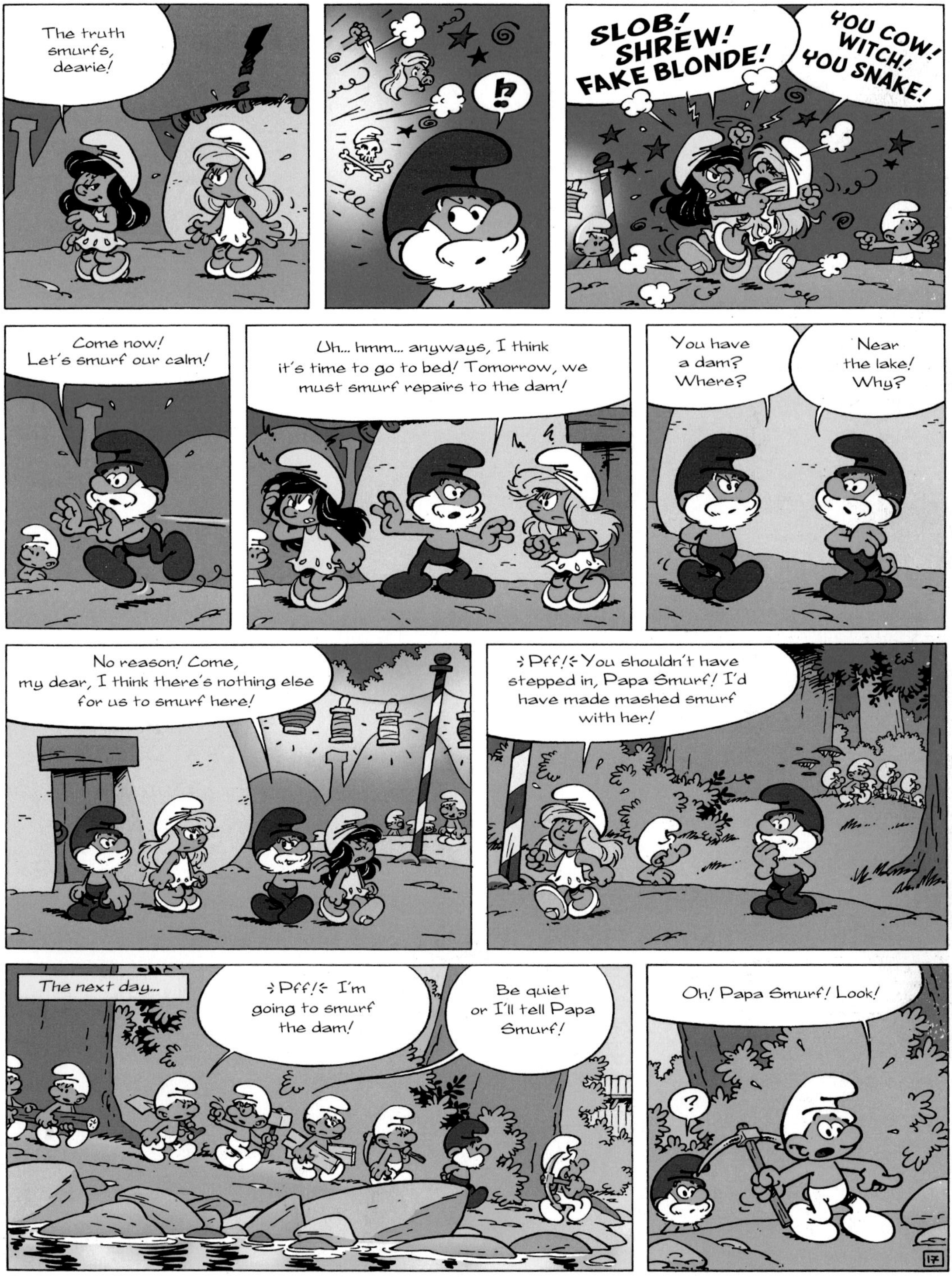

The truth smurfs, dearie!
!
!?
SLOB! SHREW! FAKE BLONDE!
YOU COW! WITCH! YOU SNAKE!
Come now! Let's smurf our calm!
Uh... hmm... anyways, I think it's time to go to bed! Tomorrow, we must smurf repairs to the dam!
You have a dam? Where?
Near the lake! Why?
No reason! Come, my dear, I think there's nothing else for us to smurf here!
Pff! You shouldn't have stepped in, Papa Smurf! I'd have made mashed smurf with her!
The next day...
Pff! I'm going to smurf the dam!
Be quiet or I'll tell Papa Smurf!
Oh! Papa Smurf! Look!
?
17

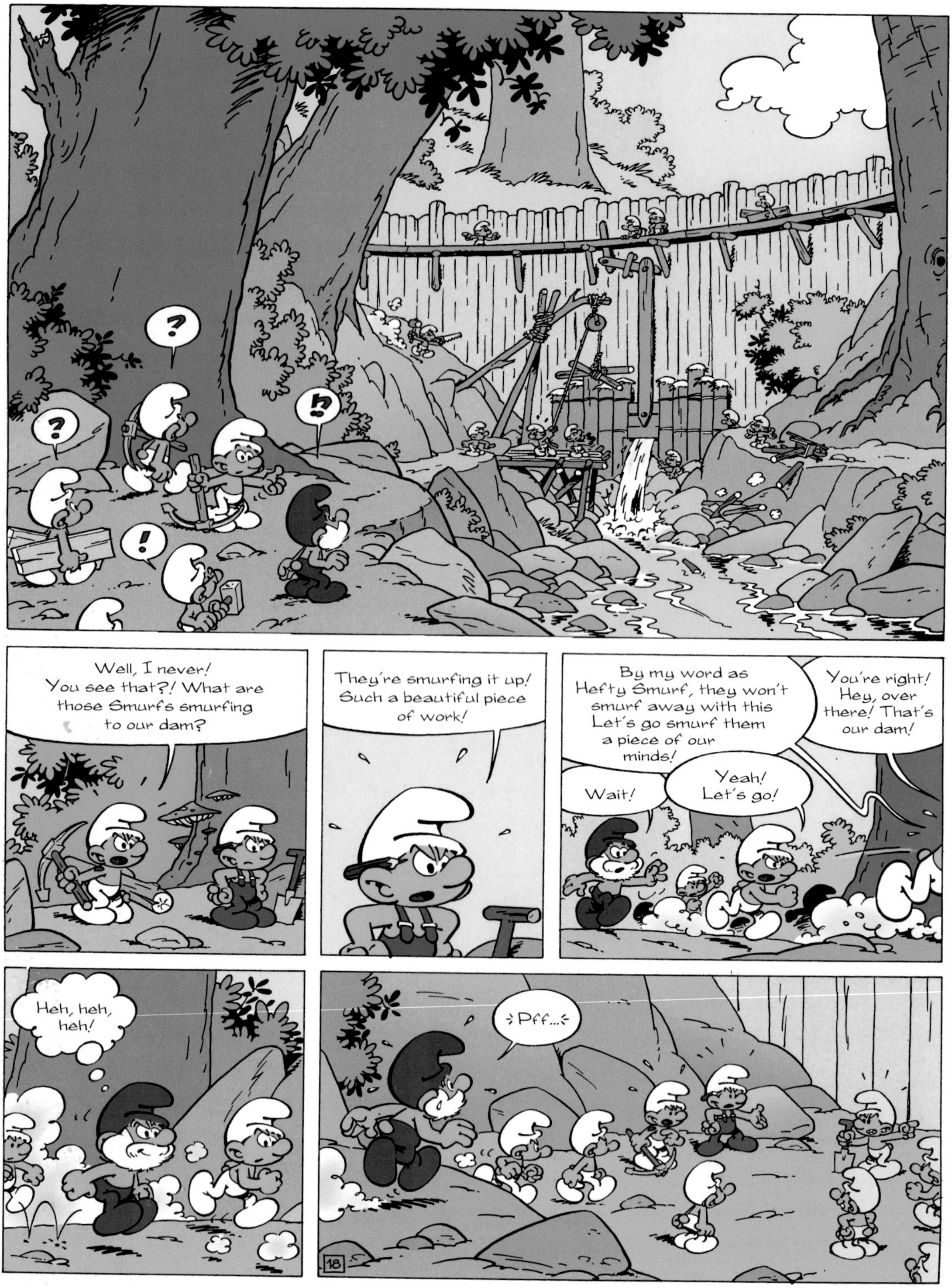
?
?
!?
!
Well, I never! You see that?! What are those Smurfs smurfing to our dam?
They're smurfing it up! Such a beautiful piece of work!
By my word as Hefty Smurf, they won't smurf away with this Let's go smurf them a piece of our minds!
You're right! Hey, over there! That's our dam!
Wait!
Yeah! Let's go!
Heh, heh, heh!
Pff...
18

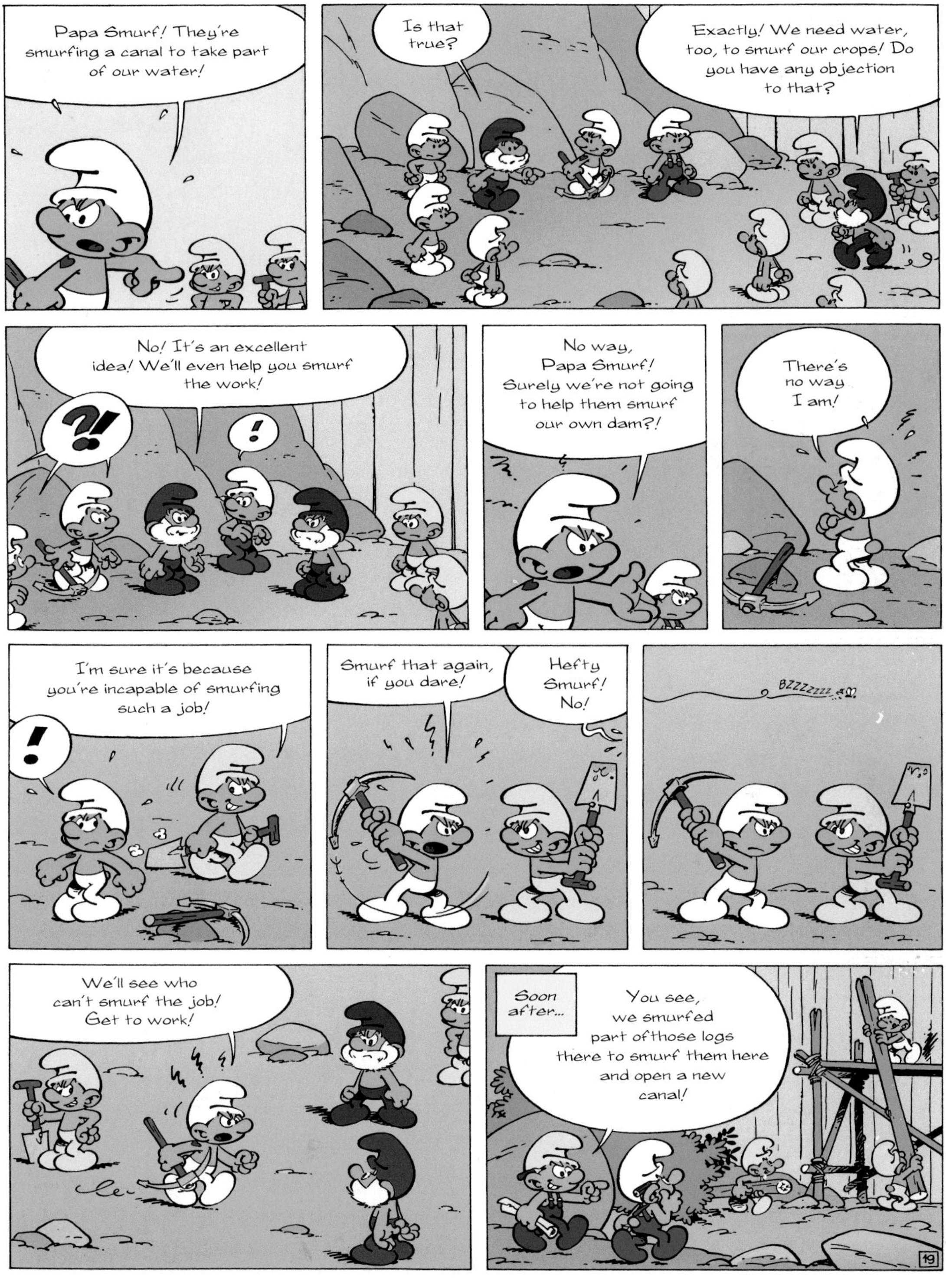
Papa Smurf! They're smurfing a canal to take part of our water!
Is that true?
Exactly! We need water, too, to smurf our crops! Do you have any objection to that?
No! It's an excellent idea! We'll even help you smurf the work!
?!
!
No way, Papa Smurf! Surely we're not going to help them smurf our own dam?!
There's no way I am!
!
I'm sure it's because you're incapable of smurfing such a job!
Smurf that again, if you dare!
Hefty Smurf! No!
BZZZzzzz
We'll see who can't smurf the job! Get to work!
Soon after...
You see, we smurfed part of those logs there to smurf them here and open a new canal!
19

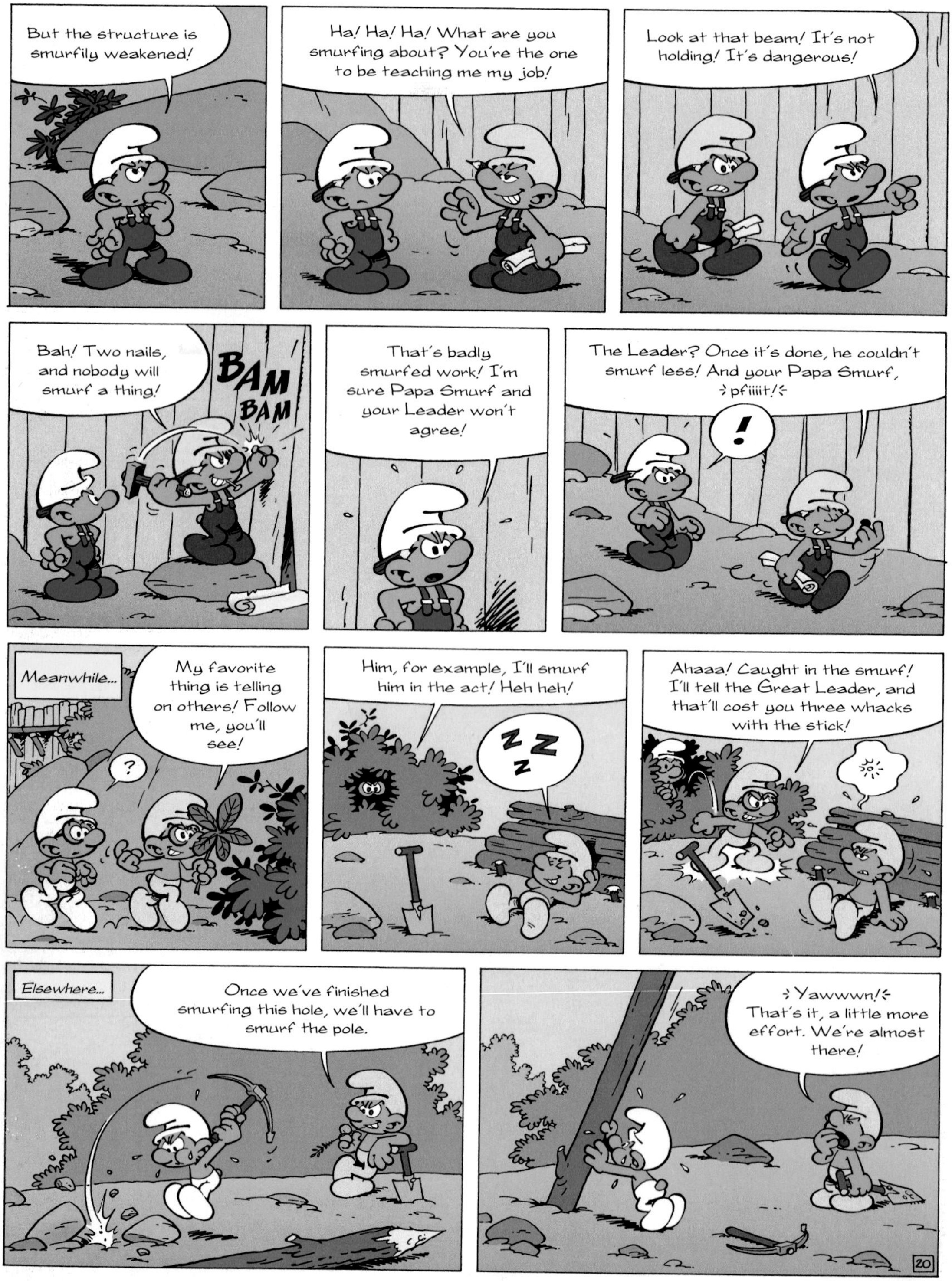
But the structure is smurfily weakened!
Ha! Ha! Ha! What are you smurfing about? You're the one to be teaching me my job!
Look at that beam! It's not holding! It's dangerous!
Bah! Two nails, and nobody will smurf a thing!
BAM BAM
That's badly smurfed work! I'm sure Papa Smurf and your Leader won't agree!
The Leader? Once it's done, he couldn't smurf less! And your Papa Smurf, pfiiiit!
!
Meanwhile...
My favorite thing is telling on others! Follow me, you'll see!
?
Him, for example, I'll smurf him in the act! Heh heh!
Z Z Z
Ahaaa! Caught in the smurf! I'll tell the Great Leader, and that'll cost you three whacks with the stick!
Elsewhere...
Once we've finished smurfing this hole, we'll have to smurf the pole.
Yawwwn! That's it, a little more effort. We're almost there!
20

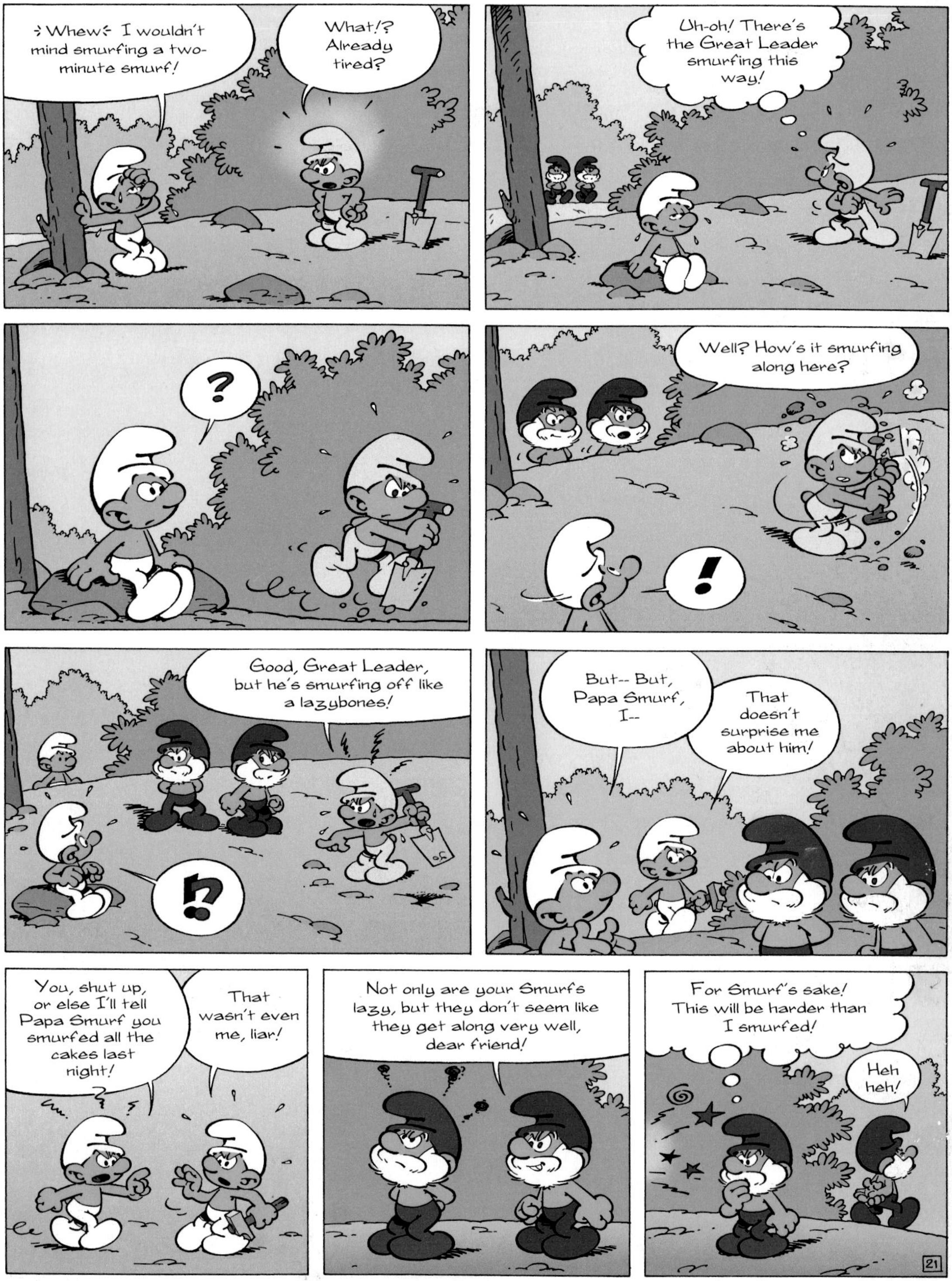

Whew I wouldn't mind smurfing a two-minute smurf!
What!? Already tired?
Uh-oh! There's the Great Leader smurfing this way!
?
Well? How's it smurfing along here?
!
Good, Great Leader, but he's smurfing off like a lazybones!
But-- But, Papa Smurf, I--
That doesn't surprise me about him!
You, shut up, or else I'll tell Papa Smurf you smurfed all the cakes last night!
That wasn't even me, liar!
Not only are your Smurfs lazy, but they don't seem like they get along very well, dear friend!
For Smurf's sake! This will be harder than I smurfed!
Heh heh!
21

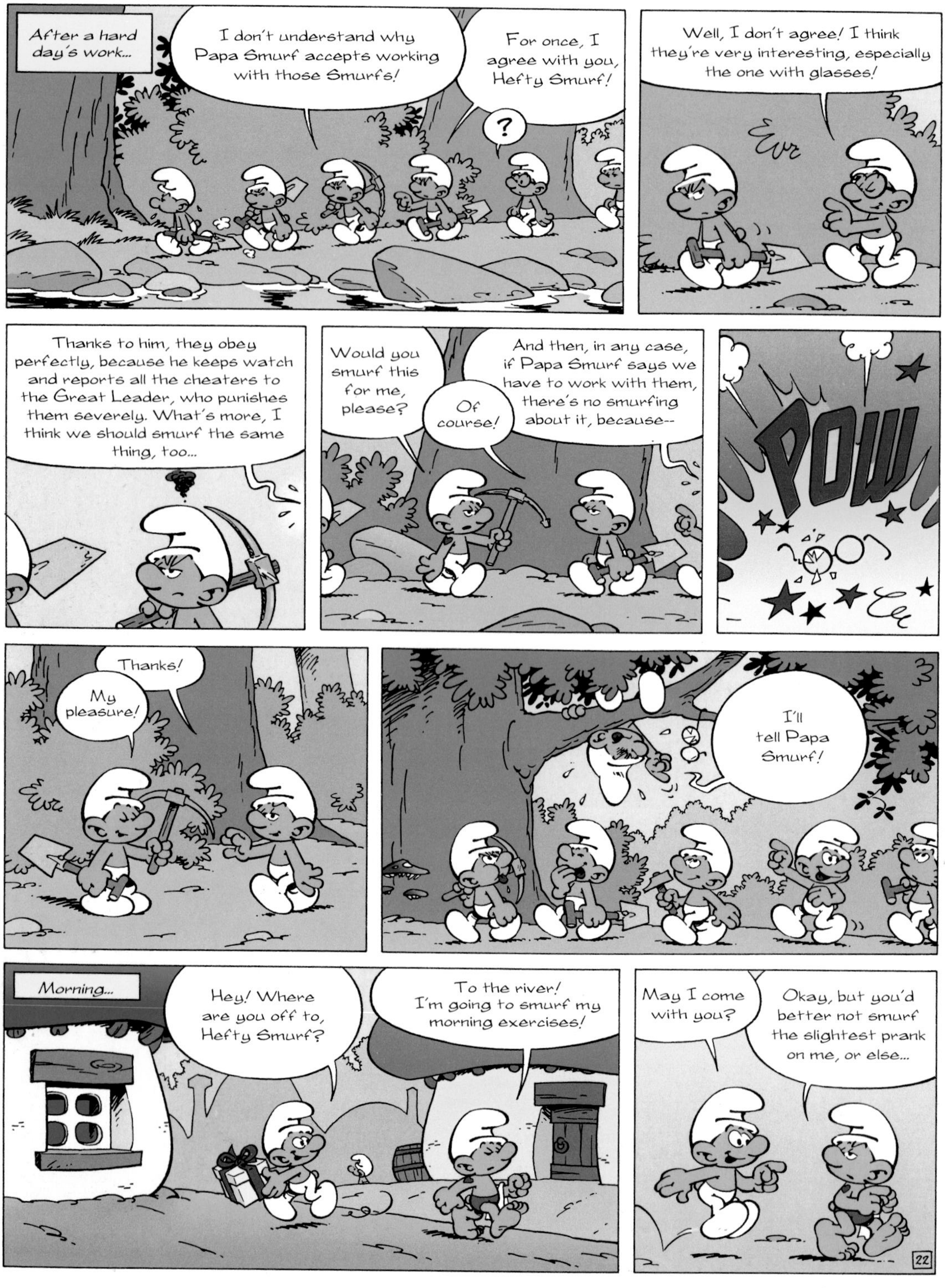
After a hard day's work...
I don't understand why Papa Smurf accepts working with those Smurfs!
For once, I agree with you, Hefty Smurf!
?
Well, I don't agree! I think they're very interesting, especially the one with glasses!
Thanks to him, they obey perfectly, because he keeps watch and reports all the cheaters to the Great Leader, who punishes them severely. What's more, I think we should smurf the same thing, too...
Would you smurf this for me, please?
Of course!
And then, in any case, if Papa Smurf says we have to work with them, there's no smurfing about it, because--
POW
Thanks!
My pleasure!
I'll tell Papa Smurf!
Morning...
Hey! Where are you off to, Hefty Smurf?
To the river! I'm going to smurf my morning exercises!
May I come with you?
Okay, but you'd better not smurf the slightest prank on me, or else...
22

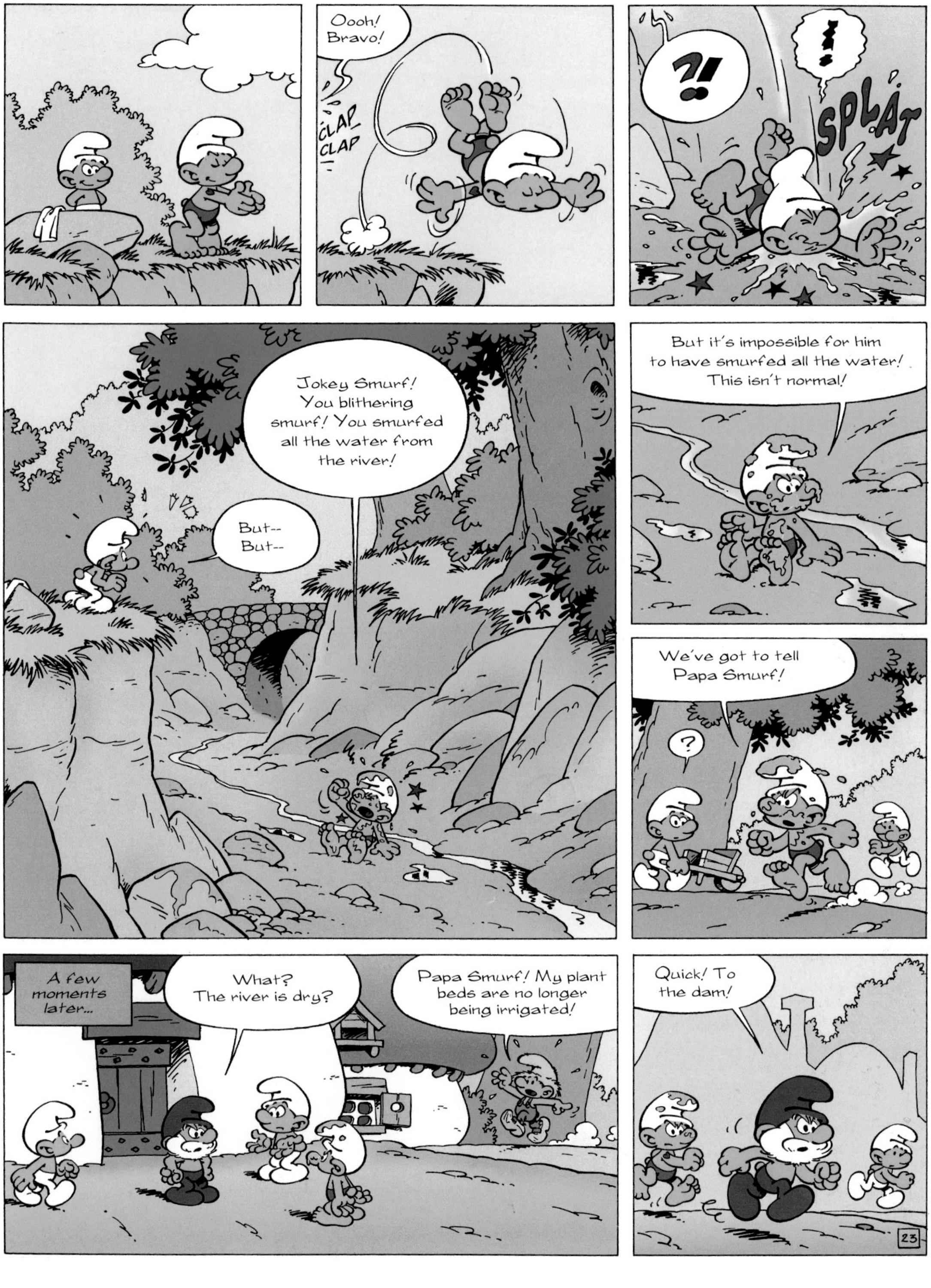
Oooh! Bravo!
CLAP CLAP
?!
SPLAT
Jokey Smurf! You blithering smurf! You smurfed all the water from the river!
But-- But--
But it's impossible for him to have smurfed all the water! This isn't normal!
We've got to tell Papa Smurf!
?
A few moments later...
What? The river is dry?
Papa Smurf! My plant beds are no longer being irrigated!
Quick! To the dam!
23

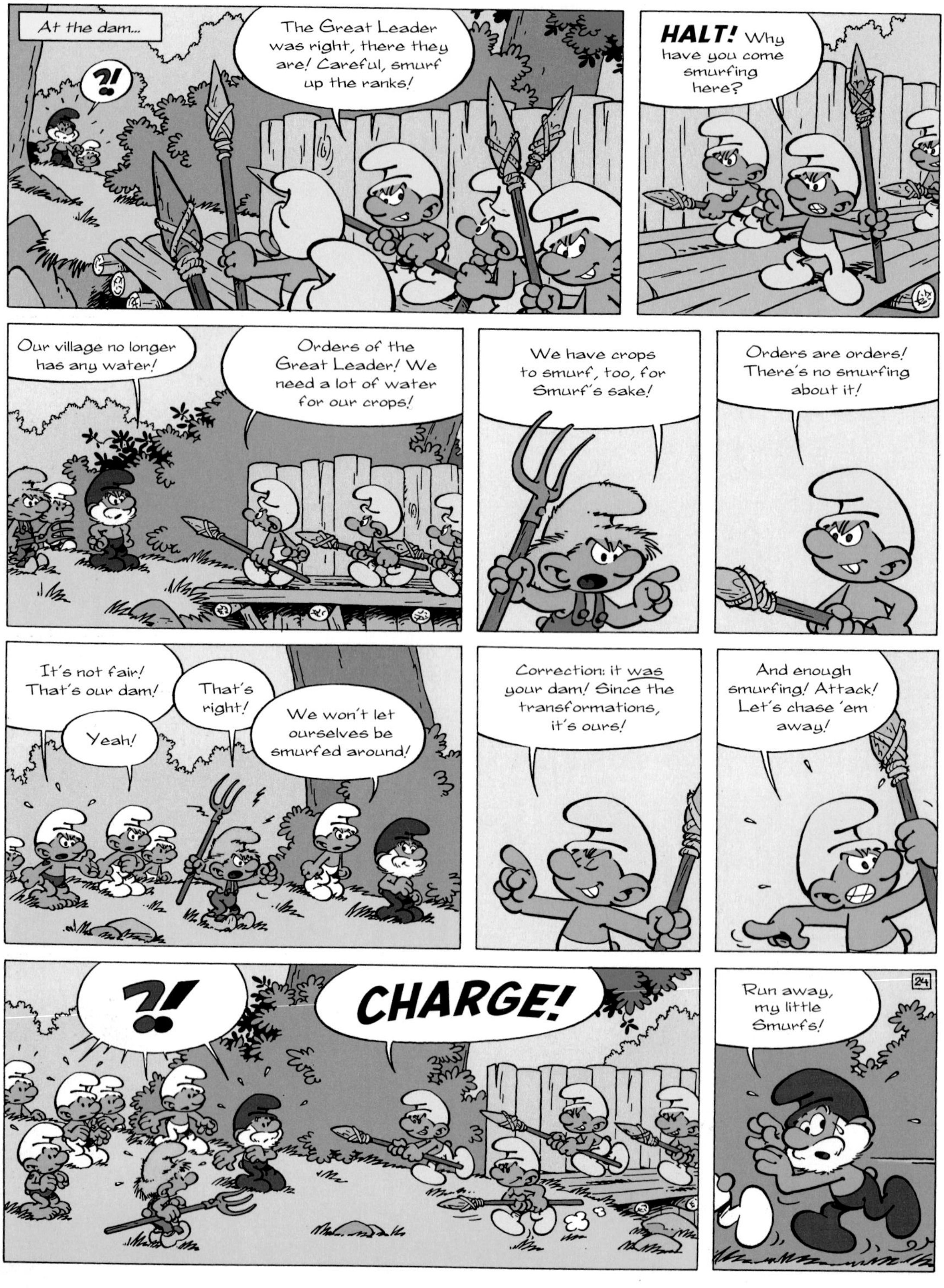
At the dam...
?!
The Great Leader was right, there they are! Careful, smurf up the ranks!
HALT! Why have you come smurfing here?
Our village no longer has any water!
Orders of the Great Leader! We need a lot of water for our crops!
We have crops to smurf, too, for Smurf's sake!
Orders are orders! There's no smurfing about it!
It's not fair! That's our dam!
Yeah!
That's right!
We won't let ourselves be smurfed around!
Correction: it was your dam! Since the transformations, it's ours!
And enough smurfing! Attack! Let's chase 'em away!
?!
CHARGE!
24
Run away, my little Smurfs!

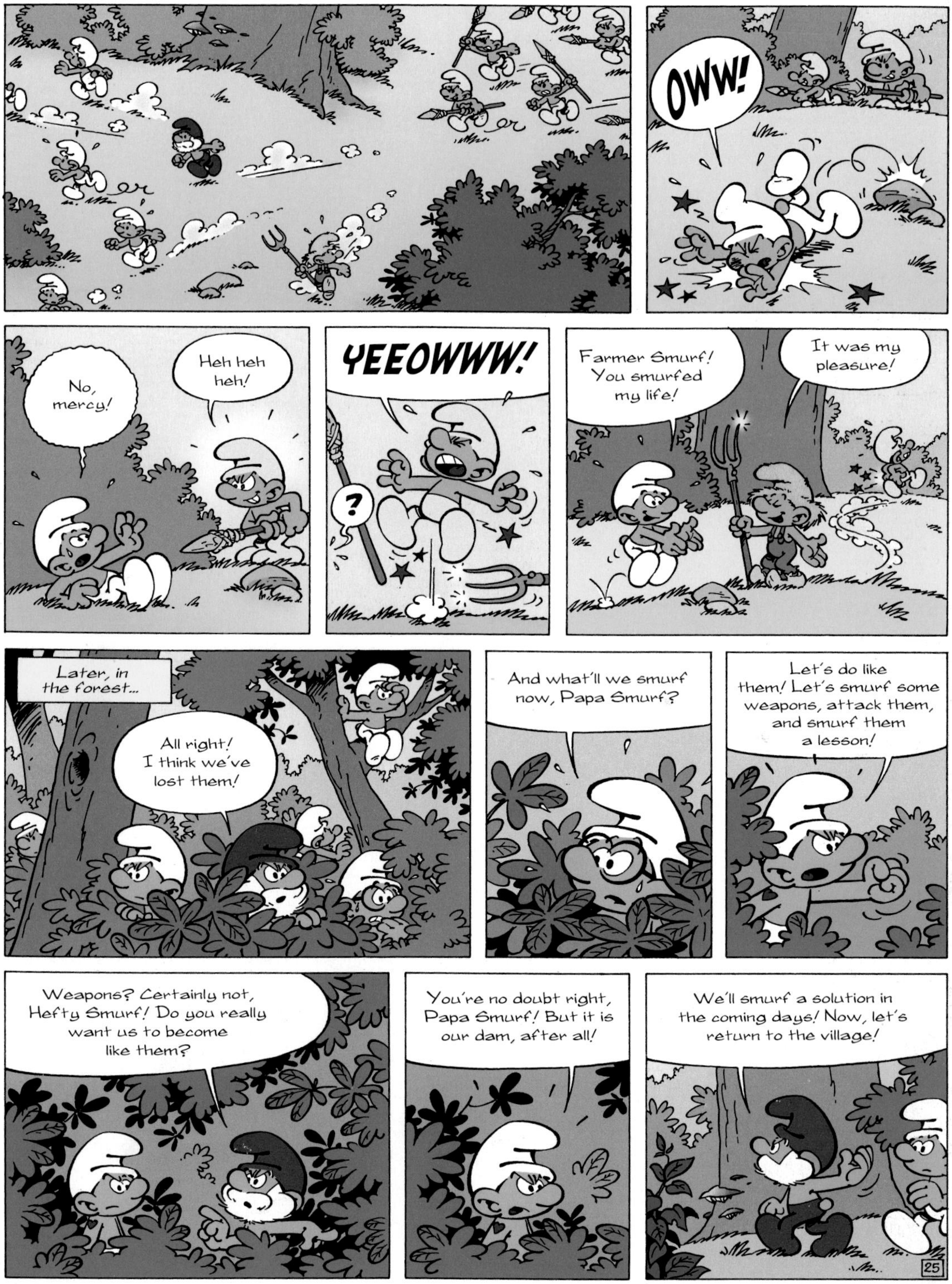
OWW!
No, mercy!
Heh heh heh!
YEEOWWW!
?
Farmer Smurf! You smurfed my life!
It was my pleasure!
Later, in the forest...
All right! I think we've lost them!
And what'll we smurf now, Papa Smurf?
Let's do like them! Let's smurf some weapons, attack them, and smurf them a lesson!
Weapons? Certainly not, Hefty Smurf! Do you really want us to become like them?
You're no doubt right, Papa Smurf! But it is our dam, after all!
We'll smurf a solution in the coming days! Now, let's return to the village!
25

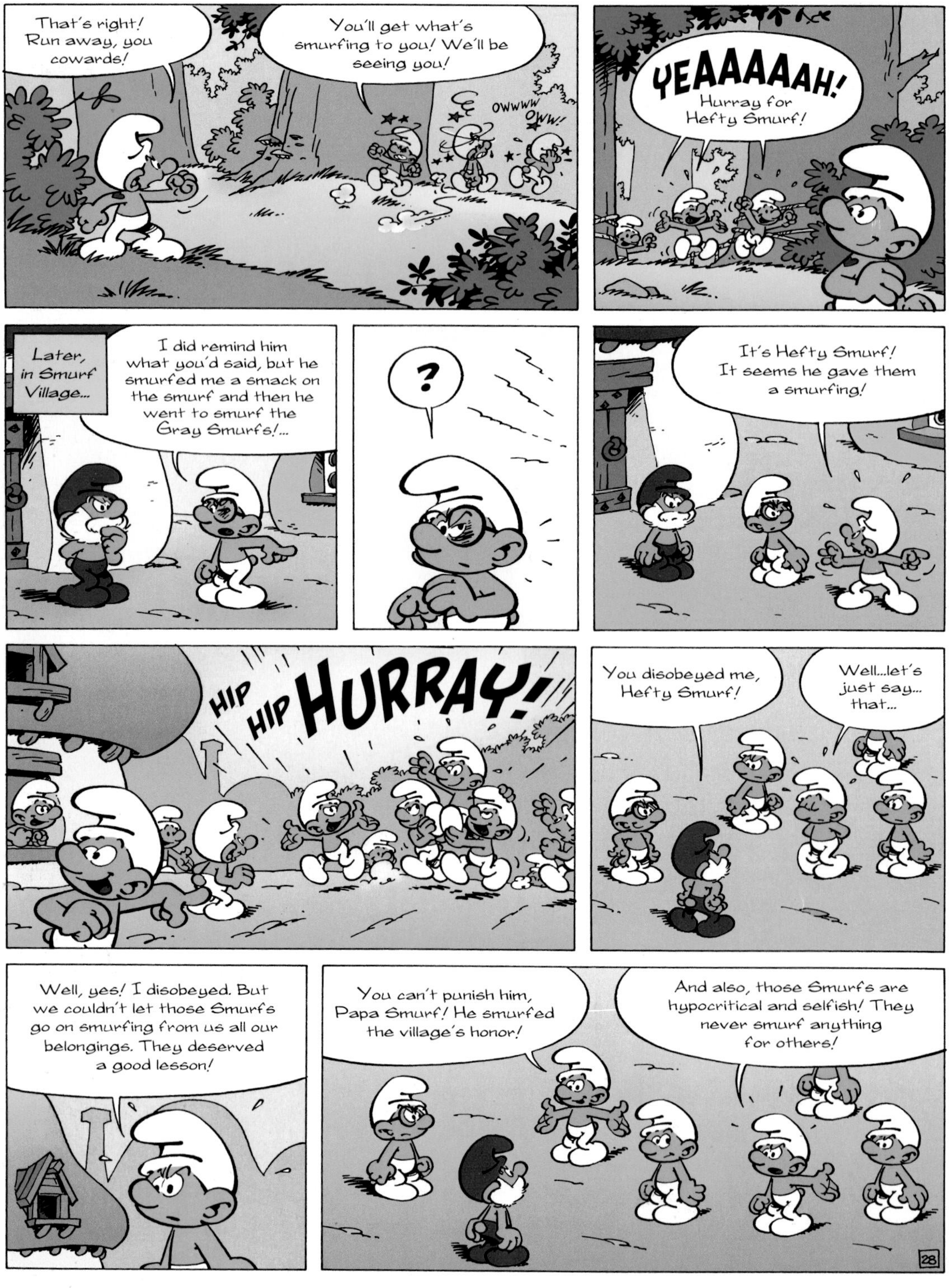
That's right! Run away, you cowards!
You'll get what's smurfing to you! We'll be seeing you!
OWWWW
OWW!
YEAAAAAH!
Hurray for Hefty Smurf!
Later, in Smurf Village...
I did remind him what you'd said, but he smurfed me a smack on the smurf and then he went to smurf the Gray Smurfs!...
?
It's Hefty Smurf! It seems he gave them a smurfing!
HIP HIP HURRAY!
You disobeyed me, Hefty Smurf!
Well...let's just say... that...
Well, yes! I disobeyed. But we couldn't let those Smurfs go on smurfing from us all our belongings. They deserved a good lesson!
You can't punish him, Papa Smurf! He smurfed the village's honor!
And also, those Smurfs are hypocritical and selfish! They never smurf anything for others!
28

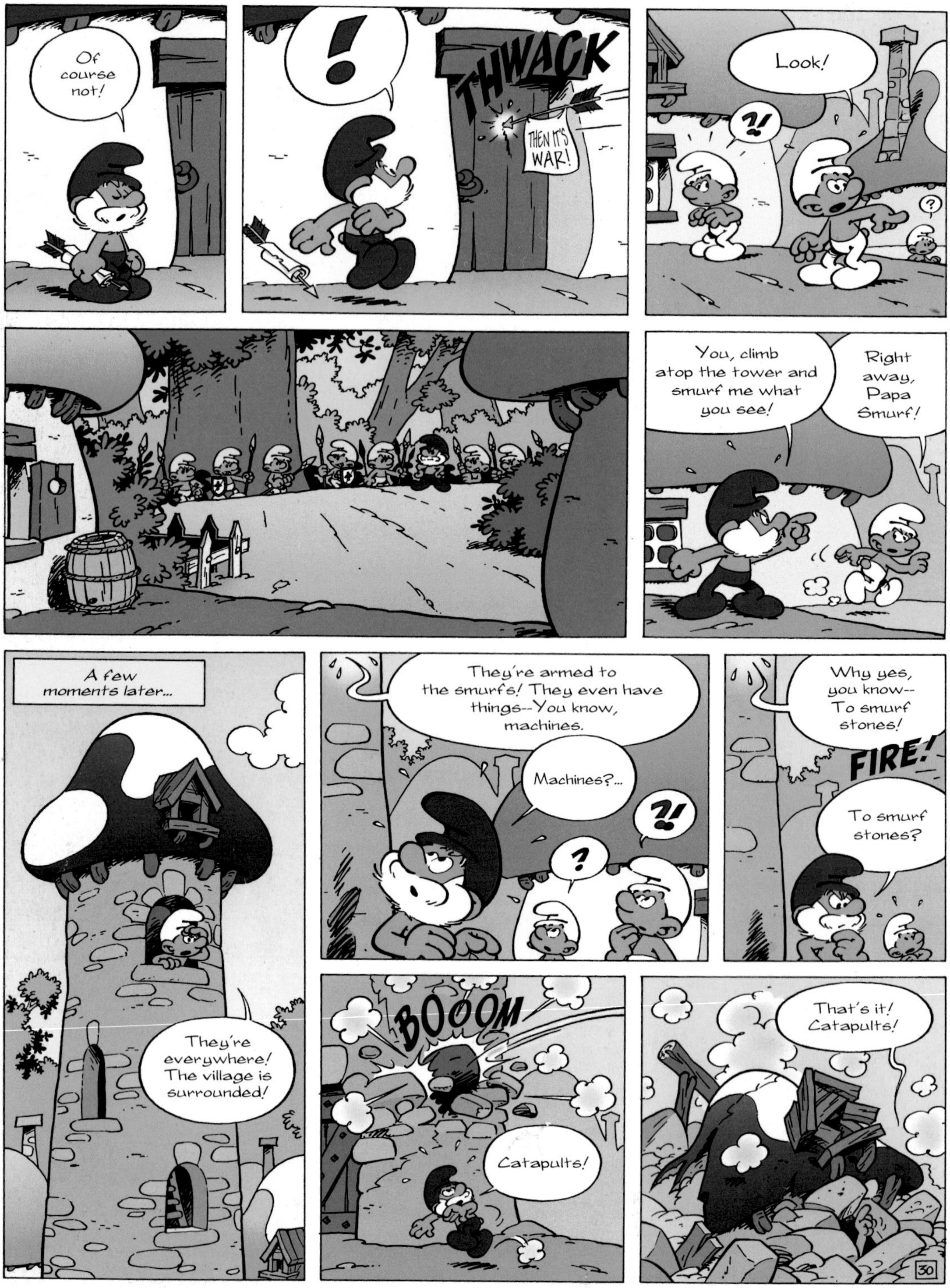

Of course not!
!
THWACK
THEN IT'S WAR!
Look!
?!
?
You, climb atop the tower and smurf me what you see!
Right away, Papa Smurf!
A few moments later...
They're everywhere! The village is surrounded!
They're armed to the smurfs! They even have things--You know, machines.
Machines?...
?!
?
Why yes, you know-- To smurf stones!
FIRE!
To smurf stones?
BOOOM
Catapults!
That's it! Catapults!
30

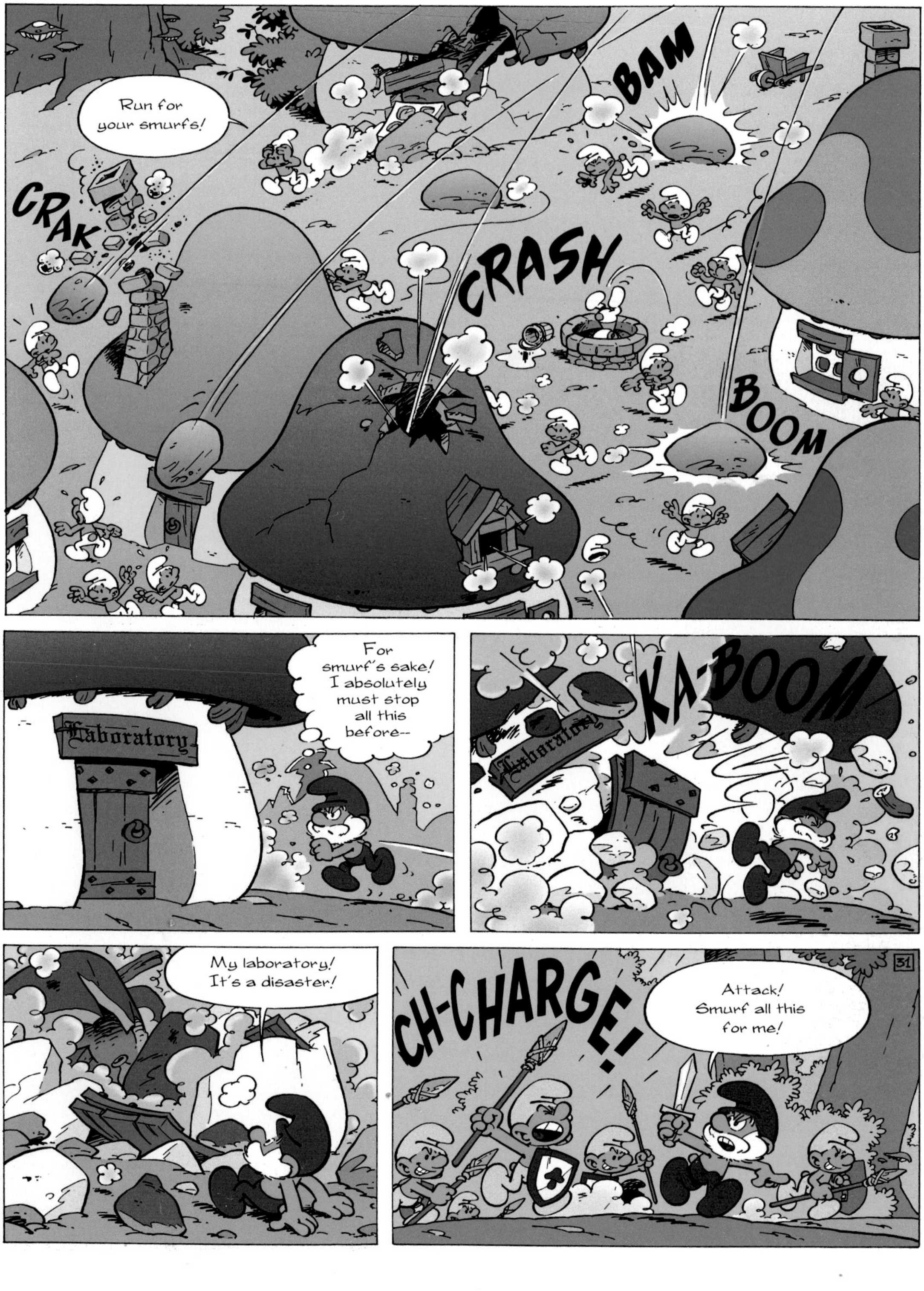
Run for your smurfs!
CRAK
BAM
CRASH
BOOM
For smurf's sake! I absolutely must stop all this before--
Laboratory
KA-BOOM
Laboratory
My laboratory! It's a disaster!
31
CH-CHARGE!
Attack! Smurf all this for me!

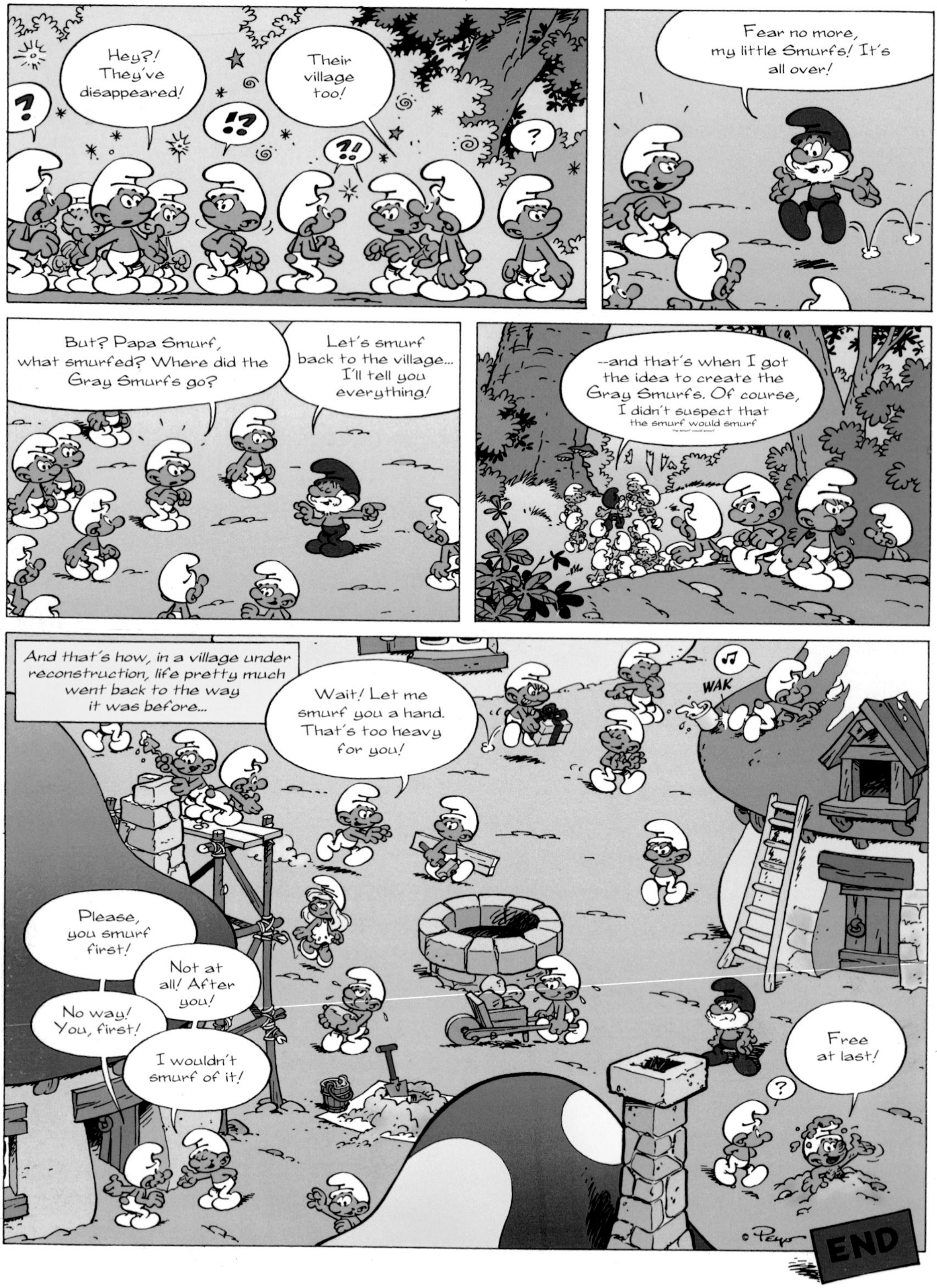
?
Hey?! They've disappeared!
!?
Their village too!
?!
?
Fear no more, my little Smurfs! It's all over!
But? Papa Smurf, what smurfed? Where did the Gray Smurfs go?
Let's smurf back to the village... I'll tell you everything!
--and that's when I got the idea to create the Gray Smurfs. Of course, I didn't suspect that the smurf would smurf
And that's how, in a village under reconstruction, life pretty much went back to the way it was before...
Wait! Let me smurf you a hand. That's too heavy for you!
WAK
Please, you smurf first!
Not at all! After you!
No way! You, first!
I wouldn't smurf of it!
?
Free at last!
© Peyo
END

THE SHADOW OF THE SMURF APPRENTICE

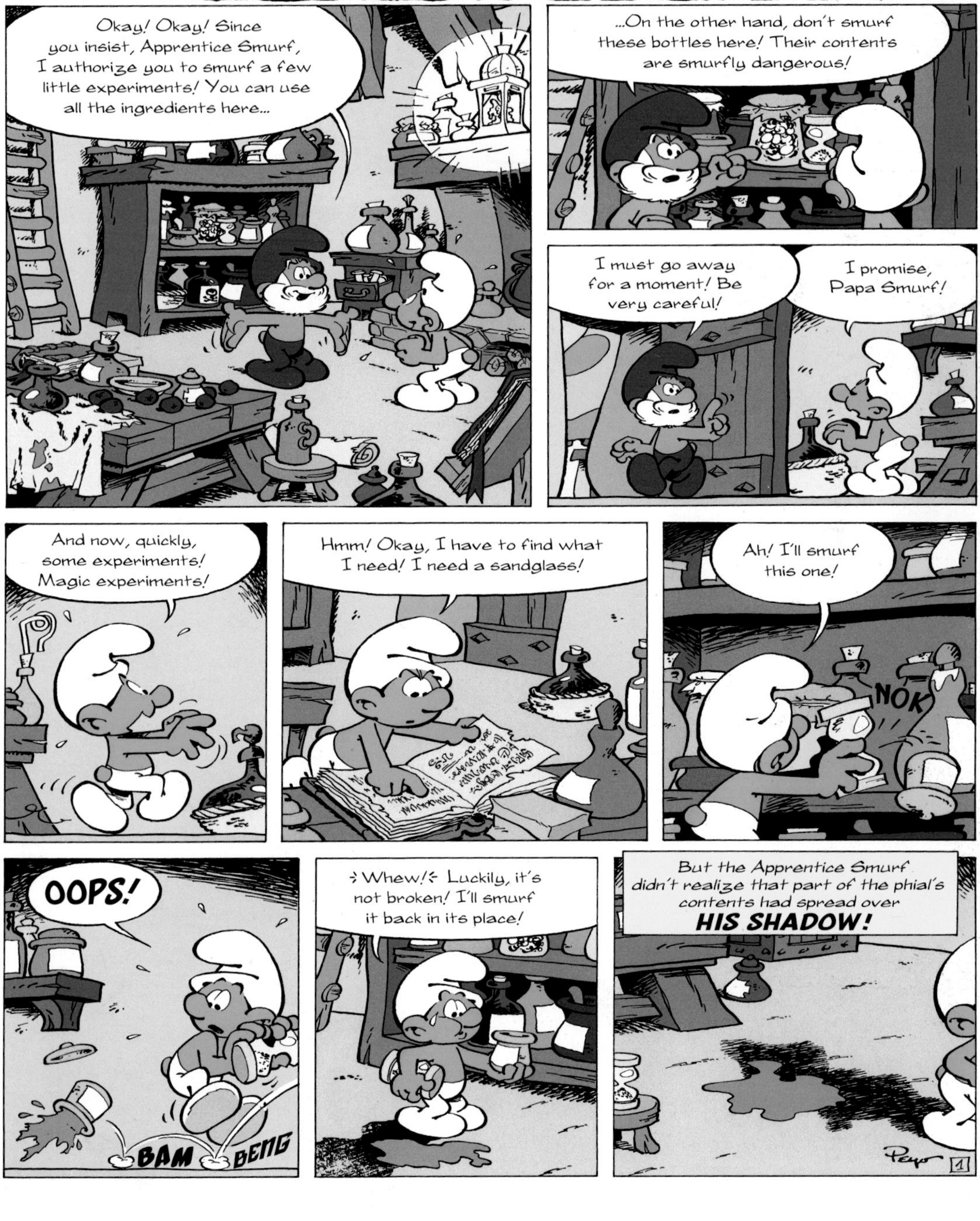
Okay! Okay! Since you insist, Apprentice Smurf, I authorize you to smurf a few little experiments! You can use all the ingredients here...
...On the other hand, don't smurf these bottles here! Their contents are smurfly dangerous!
I must go away for a moment! Be very careful!
I promise, Papa Smurf!
And now, quickly, some experiments! Magic experiments!
Hmm! Okay, I have to find what I need! I need a sandglass!
Ah! I'll smurf this one!
NOK
OOPS!
BAM
BENG
Whew! Luckily, it's not broken! I'll smurf it back in its place!
But the Apprentice Smurf didn't realize that part of the phial's contents had spread over HIS SHADOW!
Peyo
1

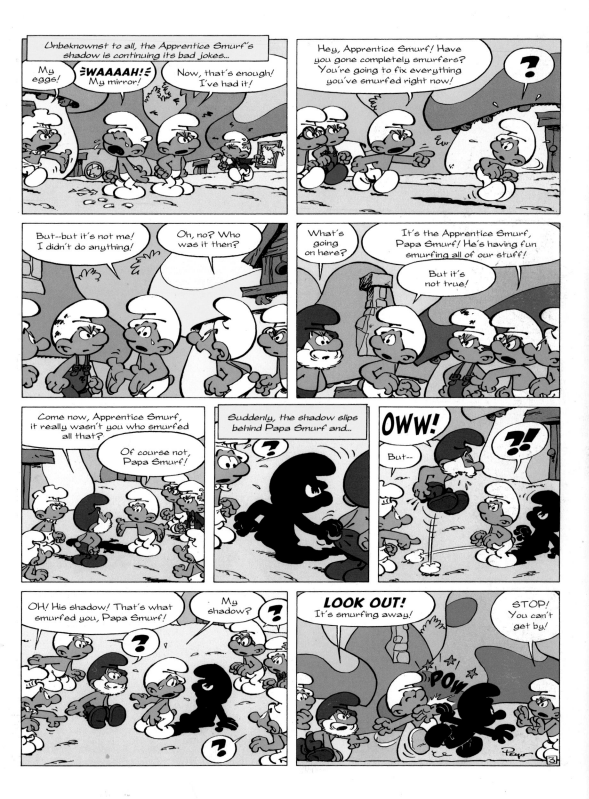

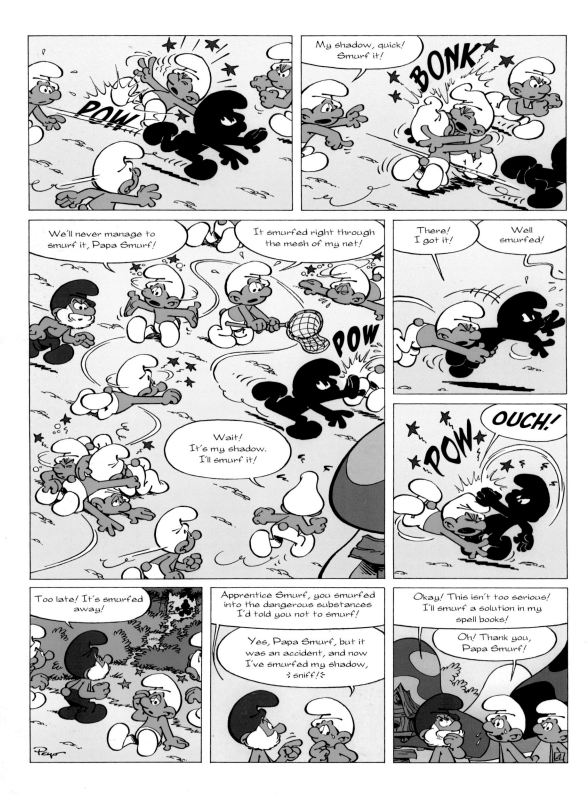

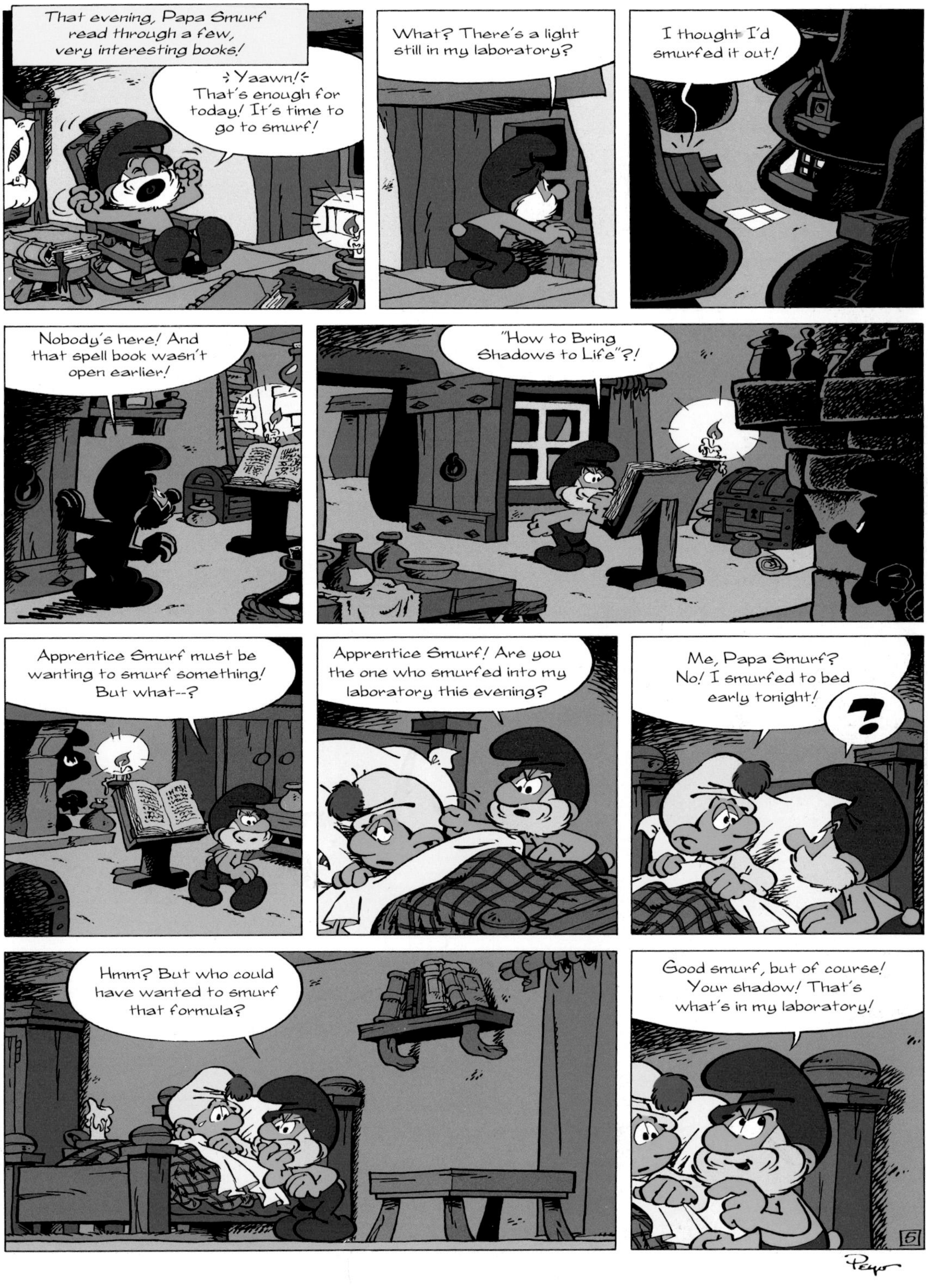
That evening, Papa Smurf read through a few, very interesting books!
Yaawn! That's enough for today! It's time to go to smurf!
What? There's a light still in my laboratory?
I thought I'd smurfed it out!
Nobody's here! And that spell book wasn't open earlier!
"How to Bring Shadows to Life"?!
Apprentice Smurf must be wanting to smurf something! But what--?
Apprentice Smurf! Are you the one who smurfed into my laboratory this evening?
Me, Papa Smurf? No! I smurfed to bed early tonight!
?
Hmm? But who could have wanted to smurf that formula?
Good smurf, but of course! Your shadow! That's what's in my laboratory!
5
Peyo

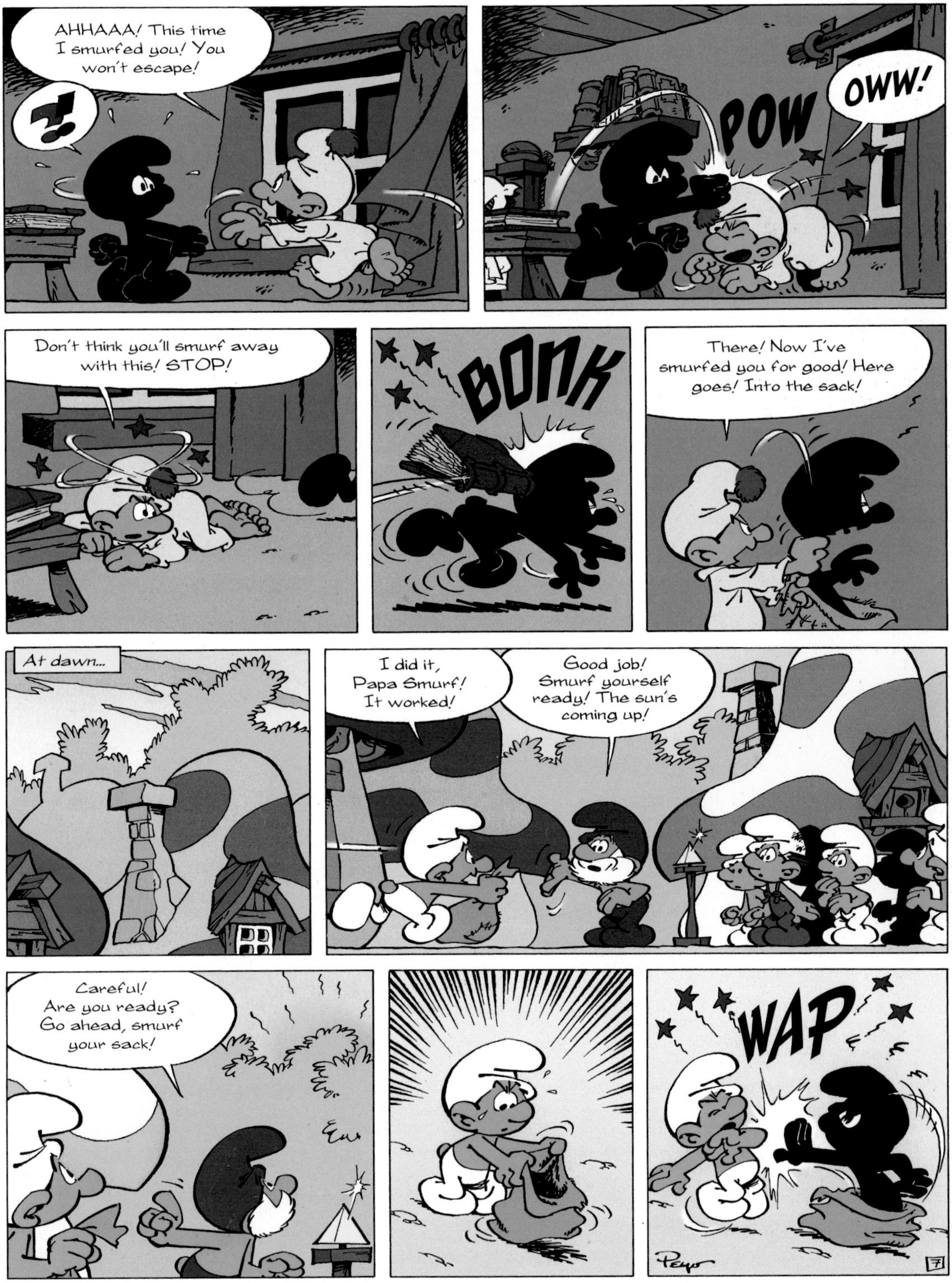
AHHAAA! This time I smurfed you! You won't escape!
POW
OWW!
Don't think you'll smurf away with this! STOP!
BONK
There! Now I've smurfed you for good! Here goes! Into the sack!
At dawn...
I did it, Papa Smurf! It worked!
Good job! Smurf yourself ready! The sun's coming up!
Careful! Are you ready? Go ahead, smurf your sack!
WAP
Peyo
7

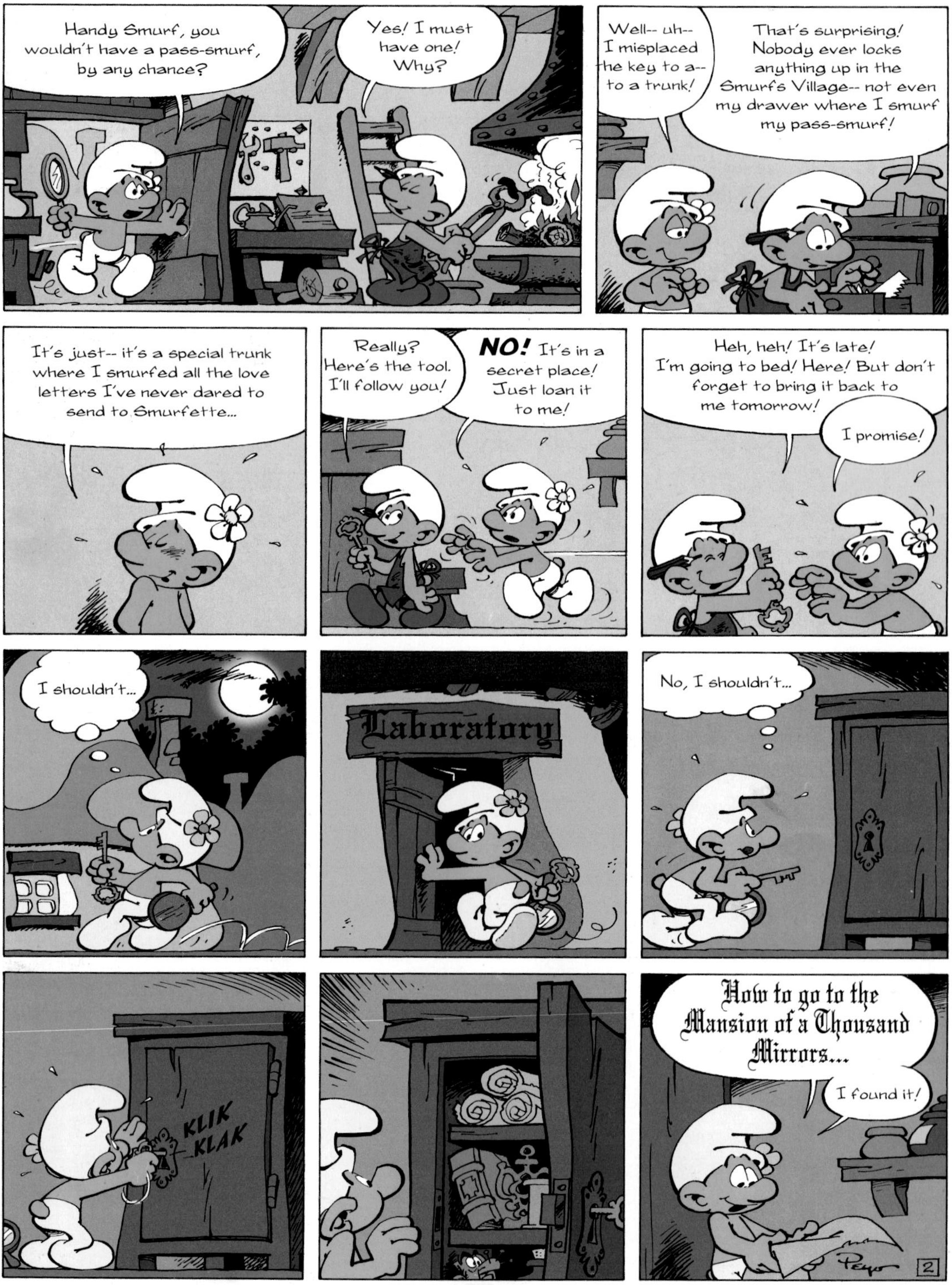

Handy Smurf, you wouldn't have a pass-smurf, by any chance?
Yes! I must have one! Why?
Well-- uh-- I misplaced the key to a-- to a trunk!
That's surprising! Nobody ever locks anything up in the Smurfs Village-- not even my drawer where I smurf my pass-smurf!
It's just-- it's a special trunk where I smurfed all the love letters I've never dared to send to Smurfette...
Really? Here's the tool. I'll follow you!
NO! It's in a secret place! Just loan it to me!
Heh, heh! It's late! I'm going to bed! Here! But don't forget to bring it back to me tomorrow!
I promise!
I shouldn't...
Laboratory
No, I shouldn't...
KLIK KLAK
How to go to the Mansion of a Thousand Mirrors...
I found it!
Peyo
2

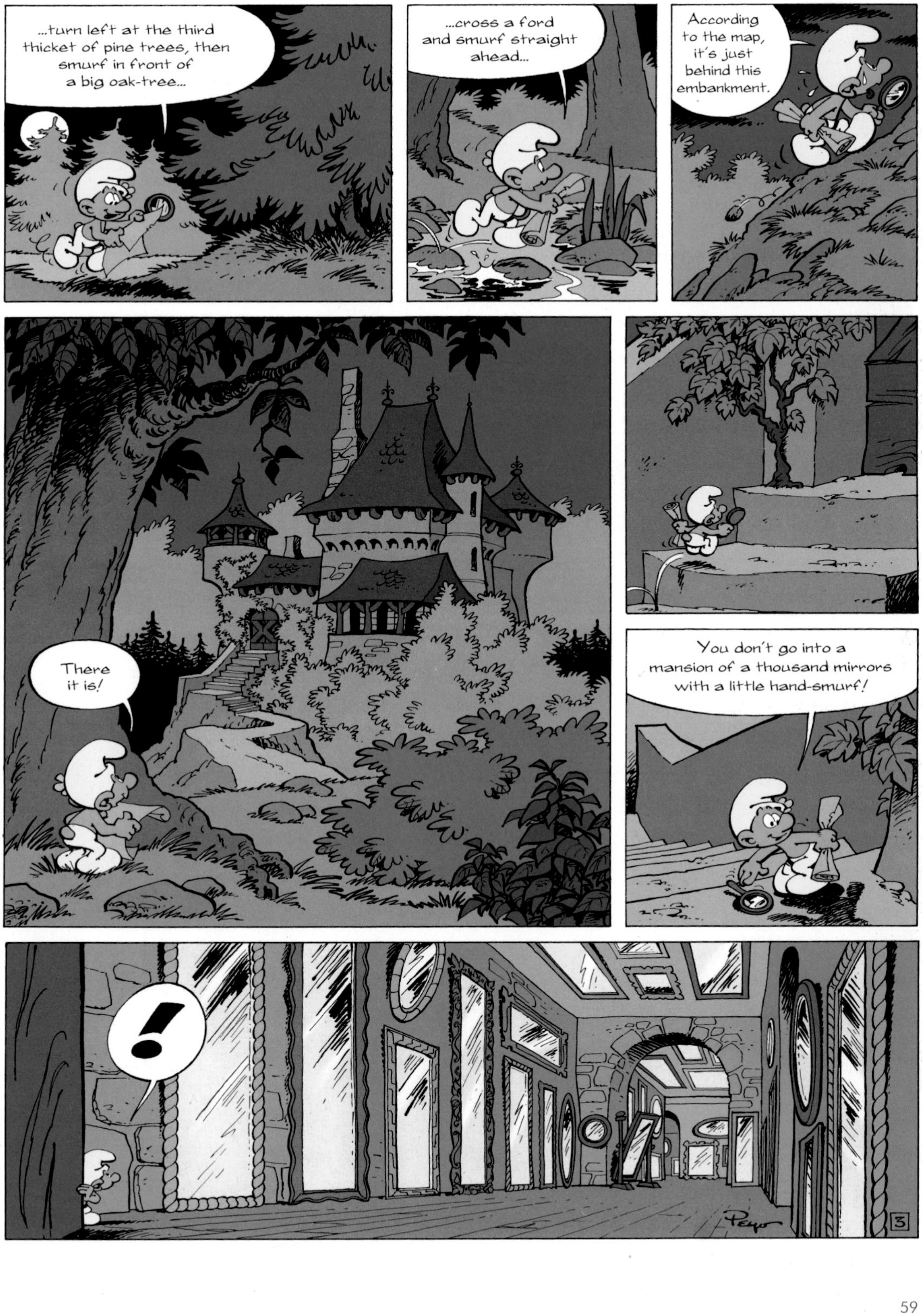
...turn left at the third thicket of pine trees, then smurf in front of a big oak-tree...
...cross a ford and smurf straight ahead...
According to the map, it's just behind this embankment.
There it is!
You don't go into a mansion of a thousand mirrors with a little hand-smurf!
!
Peyo
3

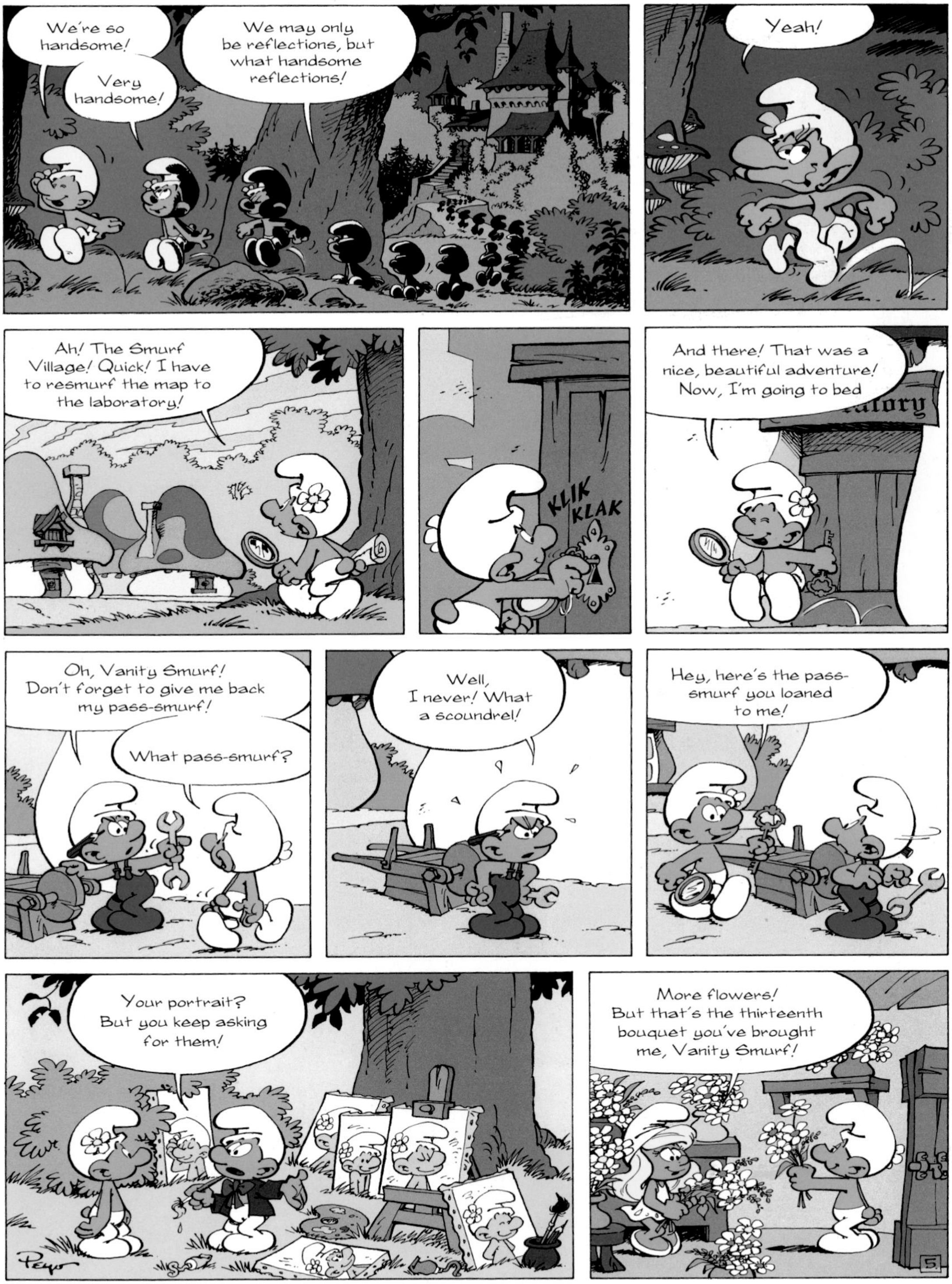
We're so handsome!
Very handsome!
We may only be reflections, but what handsome reflections!
Yeah!
Ah! The Smurf Village! Quick! I have to resmurf the map to the laboratory!
KLIK KLAK
And there! That was a nice, beautiful adventure! Now, I'm going to bed
Oh, Vanity Smurf! Don't forget to give me back my pass-smurf!
What pass-smurf?
Well, I never! What a scoundrel!
Hey, here's the pass-smurf you loaned to me!
Your portrait? But you keep asking for them!
More flowers! But that's the thirteenth bouquet you've brought me, Vanity Smurf!
Peyo
5

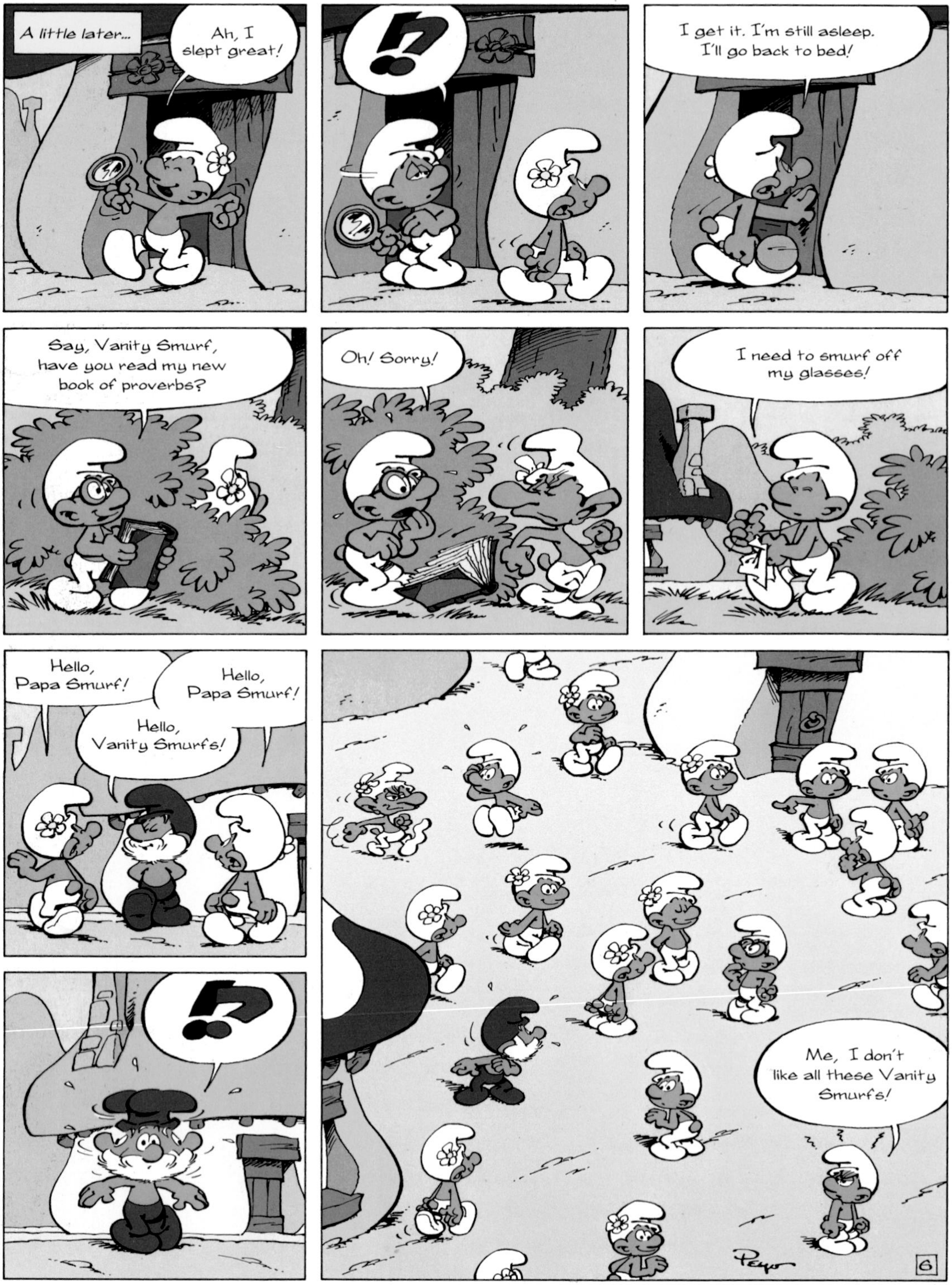
A little later...
Ah, I slept great!
I get it. I'm still asleep. I'll go back to bed!
Say, Vanity Smurf, have you read my new book of proverbs?
Oh! Sorry!
I need to smurf off my glasses!
Hello, Papa Smurf!
Hello, Papa Smurf!
Hello, Vanity Smurfs!
Me, I don't like all these Vanity Smurfs!
Peyo
6

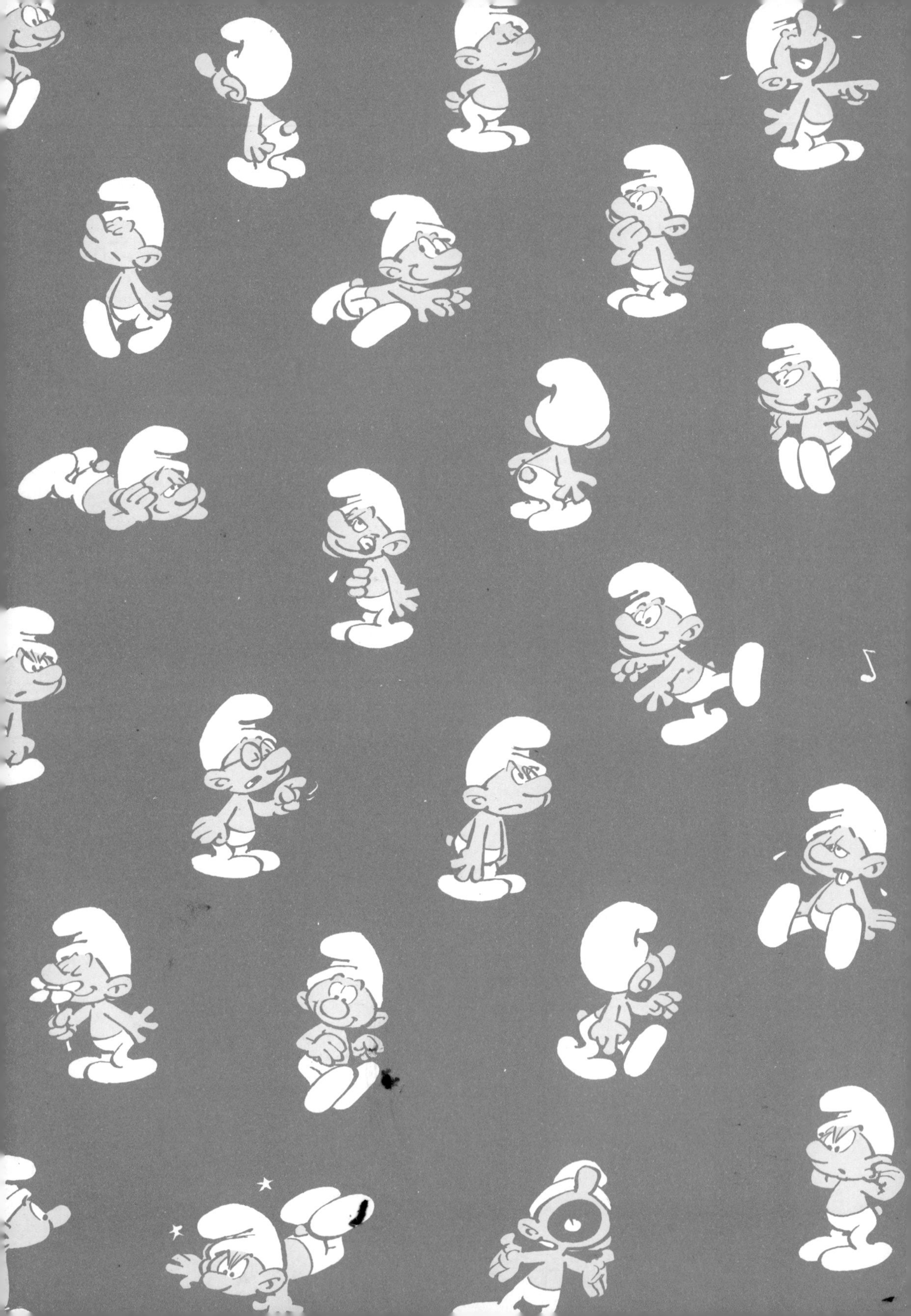